# THE ROSE CAROUSEL

Sally Rose spends her life bringing pleasure to children, but one child in particular seems to need her more than most. Little Anna, traumatized by her past and with her future threatened, requires more care than her family can provide. However, it appears that the handsome American security man in charge of her is not all he pretends to be, and Sally finds herself involved in a dangerous game to save the child and uncover the truth.

*Books by June Gadsby*
*in the Linford Romance Library:*

PRECIOUS LOVE
KISS TODAY GOODBYE
SECRET OBSESSIONS

133809

CE
LE
TEL

DR

Tel: 013

1

19

M

/

JUNE GADSBY

# THE ROSE CAROUSEL

*Complete and Unabridged*

# LINFORD
*Leicester*

First published in Great Britain in 2002

First Linford Edition
published 2004

British Library CIP Data

Gadsby, June
   The rose carousel.—Large print ed.—
Linford romance library
   1. Love stories
   2. Large type books
   I. Title
   823.9′2 [F]

   ISBN 1–84395–160–6

Published by
F. A. Thorpe (Publishing)
Anstey, Leicestershire

Set by Words & Graphics Ltd.
Anstey, Leicestershire
Printed and bound in Great Britain by
T. J. International Ltd., Padstow, Cornwall

This book is printed on acid-free paper

# 1

'Can you do that standing on your hands?' the tiny voice came and Sally gulped, trying not to look down at the little boy who was tugging at her baggy pants around knee-level.

She knew if she took her attention away from the three silver balls she was juggling in the air, she would lose control, and she had only just got the hang of it after hours of practice.

'Go away!' she hissed out of the corner of her mouth, glad her smile was painted and fixed in place by artificial means, because her real smile was beginning to droop.

'You're not very funny,' the tousle-haired lad said in a loud voice as he fingered one of her bright yellow pom-poms. 'Are you a real clown?'

Sally hesitated just a fraction of a second and that was enough. Down came the balls, one of them hitting her between the eyes and making her see stars. She had to bluff it out and pretended that dropping the balls was all in the act, which sent the other children into hysterics. They all scattered, running after the balls and bringing them back to her in their sticky, eager little hands.

Oh, well, it couldn't go on for ever, this business of being a clown. Either Rob would recover from his sprained ankle soon or they would have to hire someone else from the local theatrical agency.

It was hardly fitting for the owner of The Rose Carousel to be cavorting in the park dressed as JoJo the Clown.

Sally did a few, clumsy dance steps, glad that JoJo was not known for being a latter-day Fred Astaire, because she was certainly not Ginger Rogers. Dancing at discos was fine, and she could even manage some basic modern ballroom, but combining dancing to athletic tumbling was a little beyond her. Well, more than a little, actually.

'Now then, children!'

It was time to go into her last daily spiel, which she always looked forward to because it meant she was nearly finished and she could stop being JoJo and go back to being Sally Rose.

'Do you know what JoJo has here in his bag?' she continued.

'You're not JoJo! You're a girl!'

The little boy was back again, his pugnacious head thrust forward, eyes challenging. Sally growled a little under her breath, but patted his head gently anyway and turned her attention to the crowds gathering around her.

Children and parents moved in close to watch her unearth the tiny, miniature carousel that she placed on the palm of one hand. There was a buzz of voices as she pointed to it and addressed them in as sing-song a voice as she could manage. Rob was better at it. He literally sang the words to the melody of The Daring Young Man On The Flying Trapeze. Even behind her

3

clown disguise, Sally was too shy to sing in public.

'The Rose Carousel, you all know it well,' she recited. 'The music is magic, it casts a spell. Come follow me, follow me, quick as you can, I'm JoJo, the clown, the Rose Carousel man.'

Then, with a twist of the intricately-worked canopy on the carousel, she started the music-box playing. More sighs and exclamations came from the crowd of onlookers. With the music still playing, Sally handed out advertising flyers as she walked as jauntily as her tired legs would carry her, back to the shop she had made a household name in Harrogate.

She felt like the Pied Piper as she looked briefly over her shoulder, happy to see the streams of children following her, tugging eagerly at their parents, impatient to get to the real thing. It was as she headed for the main park gates that she saw him. So, he had turned up again, she thought with a little lurch of her stomach. That made five days in a row now.

As usual, he was keeping a low profile, trying to look casual and inconspicuous. That was a laugh, Sally thought. He was well over six feet tall and straight out of a fictional romance with those rugged, dark features. There was something slightly foreign about him, too. Italian, maybe? A little swarthy, but his features were classic with a touch of refinement.

Sally shrugged, dismissing him from her mind. She led her entourage out of the park and carefully across the road to where her shop, The Rose Carousel, nestled brightly between banks and solicitors' chambers — the veritable rose between thorns. But The Rose Carousel was more than just a toyshop. It was a family centre which had established itself in a very short period of time as a sort of mini-paradise for children and adults alike.

It had done so remarkably well that this year Sally had introduced a small, cosy coffee bar in one corner, and turned the back of the premises, which were quite extensive, into a crèche with a garden play area where children could be left safely while their mothers had a stress-free day shopping.

With a small, but highly-trained staff, The Rose Carousel often seemed to Sally like one big, happy, extended family. The idea made her feel good and warm inside. She had never really known her family, certainly not her parents. They had been tragically killed in a pile-up on the motorway when she was a baby.

Sally had been raised by her great-aunt, but now she was dead and all that was left in the way of relatives was her second cousin, Bella, who was fat, forty and fun to be with. Despite the difference in age, Sally being only twenty-eight, the two women got along famously. There wasn't anyone with whom Sally would rather spend time — unless he looked like that mysterious stranger in the park, but not quite so sinister, she mused as she entered the shop to a loud jangle of bells. There were more joyous shouts from the accompanying children as they scrambled for places on the grand carousel that took pride of place in the centre of the sales floor.

It wasn't, of course, a real, antique carousel, but Sally had got together with some pals from art college and they had tarted up an old fairground carousel she'd managed to buy for a song. They had painted it white and gold and piped plaster garlands of roses all around it.

A pal of Rob's who was clever with musical instruments, had fixed it up with a sort of hurdy-gurdy affair that played the old, traditional fairground music that got feet tapping and hands clapping from time to time.

'All right, you guys?'

JoJo stood at the centre of the carousel with finger poised over the starter button.

'You ready?'

'Ye-es!' the deafening response came.

JoJo, alias Sally, pressed the button and jumped off as the carousel started on its first round and the music crescendoed happily.

Sally joined Bella behind the main counter and the two women leaned on elbows, side by side, watching the new influx of special afternoon customers.

'Well, that's it. Thank goodness we don't open on Sundays,' Sally exclaimed.

'You're doing a great job, Sal,' Bella grunted with a nod. 'It's been quite a week, hasn't it?'

Sally nodded wearily.

'Mm. I suppose we shouldn't complain, but when business gets this good I sometimes wonder if I'm in the right job.'

'Maybe you should take up clowning as a career.'

'Very funny, ha! I shall be more than glad when Rob gets himself back on the job. He's a natural, whereas I have to work at it and acting the fool in public is not what I was put on this earth for.'

'Go on with you, Sal. You love it, really! I've watched you around the kids. You simply lap it up.'

Sally shook her head and there was a slight sadness in her eyes that her smile did not disguise.

'Not really, Bella. I love children, but I sometimes wonder if I'm rubbing salt into old wounds by doing all this. You know, why a toy shop?'

Bella had noticed the catch in Sally's voice. She reached out and squeezed her hand and Sally squeezed back.

'It still hurts, love, I know. Maybe it'll always hurt, but honest, you bloom when you're with children. It's your vocation.'

'I could have become a teacher.'

'You could have become lots of things, but you opted for The Rose Carousel. It's your dream, and, come on, don't kid old Bella, you love it.'

'Except when I feel tired and menaced.'

'Tired I can understand, but what's this menaced bit?'

Sally turned and now leaned backward against the counter, pulling off her stained gloves and removing her false red nose which was pinching as painfully as the outsized black patent shoes she had strapped to her feet.

'He was there again today, Bella.'

'What? Your mysterious stalker?'

Bella had had a daily report of the tall, dark stranger who lurked in the park when Sally, as JoJo, was performing. Sally nodded.

'Well, he's not a stalker, exactly. He just stands there and watches me and his eyes travel over the children all the time. It's weird.'

'Maybe he's just a fellow who likes children. Some do, you know.'

Sally knew her cousin was getting in a subtle dig, thinking of the two men in Sally's life so far. Sally thought of them, too, quite often, and the thought depressed her. The first had been when she was still at art college. He was a good bit older than she was, good looking, lots of charisma, great with his students. He had been great with Sally, too, on a more personal level. They even got engaged. Then she discovered he didn't like children, wouldn't father one to save his life.

That was a blow to the twenty-year-old Sally whose dream, old-fashioned though it sounded these days, was to get married and have children who would know the joys of childhood, childhood she knew existed, but had never experienced herself because her aunt had been so strict and straight-laced and thought that childhood was something you had to get over like a case of measles.

The second man had swept her off her feet, mainly because she was very vulnerable after her broken engagement. He was divorced, had children, with whom he was great. When Sally married him and immediately fell pregnant, much to her delight, he was furious. He had had his fill of babies and dirty nappies, thank you very much, so what was she going to do about this disaster?

After she left him, she miscarried. It was Bella, good old Bella, who had rallied round and picked up the pieces, fitting them together again until Sally was once more whole. And with money left her by her aunt, she opened The Rose Carousel and never looked back. She might get lonely from time to time, but she never hungered after marriage. After her past experiences, how could she trust any man? The children who came regularly into her emporium were family enough.

'Sal!'

Bella was digging her surreptitiously in the ribs through her blue, yellow and red satin costume.

'Don't look now, but I think your lurker has just come into the shop.'

Sally gave a quick glance over her shoulder. He was just closing the door, so his head was turned from her, but she couldn't mistake that build. It was him all right. There wasn't another man in Harrogate who looked like that and wore expensive suits and designer shirts. She gasped and slid swiftly down to the floor behind the counter.

'What are you doing down there?' Bella whispered and gave a nervous giggle as Sally started to inch her way on her knees towards the staff restroom at the back of the shop. 'Come back, you fool! Oh — er — good afternoon, sir! What can I do for you?'

'I'm looking for a clown who came in here,' a deep, dark brown voice came to Sally's ears, a pleasant sound with an American accent. 'I believe he's called JoJo and he works for you.'

Sally froze, not daring to move a muscle. As long as Bella stayed where she was there was a chance that he would not see her crouching there on all fours. She groaned inwardly. If only she had been quicker and made it to the restroom. She could have changed and he would never have known who she was. Not that he would know anyway, because she had no intention of meeting him, either as Sally or as

13

JoJo. There was something about him that scared her, something that didn't bear thinking about.

'Yes,' Bella was blustering, probably waving her plump arms in the air the way she did when she was excited or nervous. 'Yes, I suppose you could say that the clown works for us — he — er — oh! Excuse me, sir!'

Sally was aware of Bella moving sideways like a crab. She held her breath until she thought she would go blue in the face, then opened her eyes to see a pair of elegant, highly-polished shoes planted inches away from her nose.

'JoJo, I presume,' the voice said and her eyes started the climb up the tremendous length of male legs.

'Nice shoes!' she said, blushing scarlet beneath her make-up.

She scrambled to her feet with difficulty, then almost fell over because her own outsize JoJo shoes had come adrift. A pair of large, strong hands grabbed her, steadied her, and remained clamped on her upper arms.

'Really, sir!' Bella said, trying to insert herself between them, but wasn't being very effective for one reason or another. 'If it's something in the toy line you're looking for, I'm sure I can help. JoJo is just our advertising clown, a gimmick, you might say. He brings in the customers.'

'So I've noticed.'

Without her elevated shoes and sagging inside her clown suit, Sally felt like the incredible, shrinking woman. She put her head back and looked up into the face that had haunted her every day for nearly a week. He was even better looking on close scrutiny. A little older, perhaps, than she had imagined, but the extra years only served to make him more interesting. And his eyes were like dark crystals, cold and fathomless — and dangerous, she decided, as her stomach and her heart did a crazy loop-the-loop in tandem.

'Whatever it is you want,' Sally said, trying to keep her voice steady, though she couldn't for the life of her think why it should tremble so much, 'Bella will be able to help you.'

'You're not the real JoJo,' he said, after a moment's hesitation. 'What happened to the original clown?'

Sally blinked up at him, licking dry lips and realising that her ears were probably lighting up since he still had her arms clamped tightly to her side where the contact switch was.

'He sprained his ankle. Fell off his mono-cycle when a child put a spoke in his wheel.'

'Ah, I see.'

His vice-like grip slackened and she pulled away as he turned back to Bella, who was frantically signalling by pointing at her own ear. Sally caught a glimpse of herself reflected in a mirrored pillar a few feet away. Somehow, the tall, dark American had set off a short in her electrical system. Her ears weren't only lit up — they were flashing like neon signs!

In one swift moment, Sally dragged

16

the ears off with a painful wince and a squeak that she couldn't restrain. She thought she saw the stranger's mouth twitch at the corners. Had he almost smiled? She was curious to know what he looked like without that serious scowl on his face.

'My name's Gavin Calder,' he said, taking out a rather official identity card that claimed he was Gavin Calder of Calder Security Enterprises, Inc., Chicago, U S A.

Well, Sally thought, he certainly looked the part. If we were back in the Thirties he would probably be wearing a striped suit and white spats.

'What can we do for you, Mr Calder?' she said, stuffing her oversized ears into her deep pockets.

'I'd like to speak to the owner of this establishment. That would be . . . '

He glanced from Bella to Sally.

'That would be me, Mr Calder,' Sally said, proffering her hand, which he took and squeezed so hard the bones crunched. 'I'm Sally Rose.'

'I hope you're better at your real job than you are at being a clown, Miss Rose,' Gavin Calder said, then his forehead creased and he looked down at the hand she had just shaken with something of disgust in his expression.

Sally couldn't remember putting her gloves back on, but she must have done it because they were again on her hands and he was staring down in disbelief at a smear of pink toffee on his palm.

'Show Mr Calder where he can wash his hands, would you, Bella?' she said in her best employer voice kept for important clients. 'I'll see you in a few minutes, Mr Calder, after I've got myself out of this clown outfit.'

He nodded slowly, still frowning. Then Bella, with a meaningful rise of her fair, pencilled eyebrows, led him off to the customer toilets.

'Sorry about that — er — Mr Calder?' Sally apologised, still drying her hands after a quick change of clothes in the staffroom where Bella now brought the American.

'Don't mention it. It's not the first time I've had strawberry toffee to deal with.'

And, at last, he smiled. It was sudden and fleeting, but the instant his teeth flashed white, Sally felt something stir deep inside her. This was not how it was supposed to be, not with entire strangers, not with anybody.

'We can either talk here or go up to my flat which also doubles as my office.'

He looked about him and at that moment one of the childminders came in and flopped into an easy chair with a weary groan.

'Let's go to your office, shall we?' he answered.

'Yes — um — right — OK!'

Sally led the way through the back, passing through the garden section where children were playing on swings, climbing enthusiastically on frames and feeding a small collection of domestic and non-domestic animals.

'They all seem to be having a great time,' Mr Calder said, pausing to watch the various activities. 'This was all your idea, Miss . . . er . . . Rose?'

Sally nodded, smiling off into the busy distance where a group of older children were learning how to plant their own garden.

'Yes. These are some of the many things I wished I'd done as a child and never got the opportunity.'

'You must love children.'

Sally shrugged and glanced up at him in time to find his dark eyes regarding her closely, too closely for her comfort.

'Perhaps I'm just living my missing childhood through them.'

'Do they come back? I mean, do you have regular kids that you have the chance to get to know well?'

'Most of them, yes. That's been the big surprise to all of us. One or two slip through the net and are never seen again, but I'd say most of them come back when they can.'

'I'm impressed.'

'This way, Mr Calder.'

She indicated the staircase that led up to her flat above the shop. Then she started worrying about the state of the place. She couldn't remember how she had left it. She wasn't normally untidy, but from time to time things got out of hand. It was always during those times she had unexpected visitors. She opened the door and looked around tentatively. He followed her inside. She was aware that his big frame seemed to fill the tiny, cramped apartment that had once been used as a storeroom.

'Cosy!' he said.

'Small!' she countered and gave him a wry grin, then noticed that he was

21

staring at her rather hard. 'What's wrong?'

He gave a small shake of his head and again there was that devastatingly attractive smile that should have belonged to Hollywood rather than Harrogate.

'Nothing at all,' he told her after a rather audible sigh. 'I was just thinking what a pity it was to have you hidden beneath that clown disguise.'

She made a pretence of tidying up the place, plumping up cushions, shifting shiftable bits, avoiding his penetrating gaze because she could feel a rosy glow creeping up her cheeks.

'It's just temporary,' she told him, 'until Rob's well enough to get back into harness. Now, he really is good as a clown. You should see the way he can do cartwheels, and he's funny, much funnier than me.'

'Oh, I don't know.'

He was picking up photographs and inspecting them . . . Sally as a child with her aunt . . . Sally on holiday with a friend . . . Sally in a group of Art College graduates . . . Sally with Bella.

'You looked kind of cute when your ears started flashing.'

She started to laugh with him at that, but then he went on, 'No boyfriend, Miss Rose?'

She swallowed hard and shook her head.

'No boyfriend, Mr Calder, and the name's Sally, to everybody. I don't like formality.'

'That's fine. As you know, I'm Gavin. Now, Sally, can we get down to business?'

He sat down in one of her deep, cushioned armchairs. It swallowed him up and he looked all legs until he adjusted his position. When she sat down opposite, she made sure she didn't get too comfortable so as to retain a more business-like posture.

'I'm curious to know why you're here, Gavin,' she said, fixing him with a stare above her tented fingers. 'After all, you have been watching me rather closely for some days now and I must say that I've found it particularly disconcerting.'

'Yes, I'm sorry about that, but bravo! You, at least, picked me out of the crowd. I don't think your colleague did. He was the one I started watching two weeks ago.'

'Rob? Why would you want to watch him? He's a good clown, an excellent singer and dancer, but otherwise pretty harmless.'

'And careless?'

'Careless?'

'Yes. He did fall off his bike and sprain his ankle, did he not?'

Sally chuckled at that.

'Well, if you've been watching him all the time you say you have, you must know about his accident, since it happened in the park.'

'No.'

'No?'

'No. I saw no accident. Each afternoon, he did his little act in the park, then, as you did today, he led the

24

children and their parents to The Rose Carousel, all except last Saturday, when he left with a friend and drove in the opposite direction.'

Sally remembered that there had been a singular lack of the usual numbers drifting into the shop that day, and Rob had phoned to say he'd had the accident with the bike and wouldn't be in for a few days. He even apologised for not coming back to the shop to tell her, but his foot was painful and since a friend was passing at the time, he took the opportunity of getting a lift home.

'It sounds plausible,' Gavin Calder said, then studied his hands before looking up at her. 'But I didn't see him fall from his bike. However, there was a bigger crowd than usual that day and I may have been distracted. How long have you known this Rob?'

Sally didn't know why, but she was feeling a little prickly under her skin.

'I've known Rob Barlow since we were in college together, going on for

ten years. He was always more inter-
ested in theatre, so he dropped out
halfway through the first term. But we
always kept in touch.'

'On a personal level?'

'If you're suggesting a relationship,
forget it. Rob's gay and always has
been. We're friends, that's all. Everybody likes him, even when he strays a
bit.'

'Strays?'

'He — um — has a problem with low
tolerance, mild drugs, alcohol. His life
hasn't been easy, so we tend to nurse
him through the bad times when he
gets depressed.'

'Has he ever been depressed enough
to be admitted to a clinic?'

'Not to my knowledge.'

Gavin raised his head and thrust his
square chin to the ceiling at a point just
above her. Sally had to restrain herself
from looking there also in case there
was a stain or a cobweb that she had
missed.

'How far would you trust him?'

The question was addressed to the ceiling. Sally fixed her eyes on his throat. He had the neck and the shoulders of a man who worked out regularly, without being over-developed. She found herself wondering what he would look like without that suit, without the expensive shirt — in shorts, running along a beach with the sea lapping at his ankles, long legs bare. It was a very pleasing image.

'What?'

He returned his gaze to her.

'Do you trust him, Sally?'

'Yes, of course I trust Rob!'

She was beginning to get rattled by this whole meeting.

'Look, I'm sorry, but I'm rather busy. I'm tired and feeling just a little tetchy. Would you please come to the point and tell me why you're here?'

He eased himself farther up in his chair and looked as if he would like to change seats, but there wasn't another one available.

'Yes, of course. For the past few years

I've been employed as a security chief for the owner of a firm called New Galaxy Computers. My boss is American, as I am, but has been living in England for some time now. He's looking to expand his business, so he's looking at various companies with potential to do well in the states, companies with imagination, like The Rose Carousel. This is a unique enterprise, Sally. You must be proud of it.'

'Yes, I am.'

Sally was flattered but at the same time she felt wary.

'But what does all this mean in terms of business? I assume your boss is proposing some sort of business deal.'

Gavin shrugged.

'That depends. For the moment, he's looking into it on a personal level. You see, Sally, you were discovered by my boss's daughter. She's five years old and she's your most ardent fan.'

'Then I'm doubly flattered. What's her name?'

Gavin delved into his inside jacket pocket and drew out a photograph, a head and shoulders shot of a pretty little girl smiling into the camera, showing some missing teeth.

'Her name is Anna. This was taken a few weeks ago after she had been riding on your carousel.'

Sally took the photograph and stared at it for some seconds, then handed it back.

'Yes, I remember her. Delightful child, but she never spoke a word all the time she was here. For a while, we thought she was lost, but the young woman with her had just slipped out on an errand.'

Gavin's face clouded.

'The nanny, yes. Stupid girl. She wasn't supposed to let Anna out of her sight.'

'Does Anna have a problem?'

'She's the child of a wealthy business-man and was kidnapped a couple of years ago. She hasn't spoken since. Her father paid highly to get her back. He would do anything to make her happy, to hear her speak again.'

Was that a slight emotional crack she heard in Gavin Calder's voice, Sally wondered. As if he realised he was displaying too many private feelings, he cleared his throat noisily.

'I'm sorry,' Sally said, 'but I'm not sure I follow all this. Just exactly what has it to do with The Rose Carousel?'

Gavin drew in a long breath, held it, then let it out slowly. He rubbed a hand across his face and she thought he looked more weary than she felt.

'Miss Rose — Sally — I have to tell you something in strict confidence, because lives may depend on it.'

Sally shot up straight in her chair and her eyes narrowed.

'Go on,' she told him softly.

'There's been another kidnap threat. Unless I can find somewhere to hide Anna, at least on a temporary basis, her life may be in danger. Her sanity certainly is.'

'What has this to do with me, Gavin? I run a toyshop. Granted, it's a bit special as toyshops go, but . . . '

'I want you to look after Anna until the whole business is sorted out.'

'But . . . '

Sally's eyes swept her small flat wildly, not sure that what she was hearing was real.

'What about her mother? What's she doing in all this?'

'Her mother deserted her long ago. She could, of course, be at the bottom of it all. We don't know as yet. For the moment, we're keeping things quiet. No police. It would be too risky to involve them.'

'But you want to involve me — my shop — my staff!'

This was beginning to sound like fantasy land, the stuff that American movies were made of. This was Harrogate, for goodness' sake!

'I've been checking out the security. The only member of staff I had any doubts about was JoJo the clown,

31

especially when he suddenly disappeared and then reappeared some inches shorter and not so talented.'

'You don't have to be so honest, Gavin,' Sally said grittily, 'but I do know exactly where my talents lie. As far away from a three-ring circus as I can get. However, needs must when the devil drives.'

'My sentiments exactly,' he said and his mouth tilted into a lop-sided smile. 'Will you help us, Sally?'

Sally shook her head and chewed on her lip. This morning she was Sally Rose, owner of the best toyshop in Harrogate. This afternoon she made a fool of herself by acting the clown in public. This evening she was sitting opposite the most attractive, yet most scary man she had ever met and was involved in a case of threatened kidnapping.

But why did she find him so scary? What he had just told her was frightening enough in itself, but it was something more than that, something that he — his presence — did to her innermost being, like an invisible blow to her solar plexus that knocked the wind right out of her sails. No other man had produced quite the same effect.

Steady on, Sally! He's not the type to go out on a casual date, at least not with a perfectly ordinary, Yorkshire lass. He's top-model material. Nothing less would warm up the blood in those hard, masculine veins of his.

'So, Gavin,' she said a little huskily, 'where do we go from here?'

# 3

Bella was waiting downstairs with a raised eyebrow, waiting eagerly for Sally to appear.

'So?'

'So what?'

Sally shrugged, her mind working hard, trying to figure out what to say to her cousin without actually lying.

'So what happened? What did he want?'

'Oh — um — nothing very much, really.'

Bella was bursting at the seams with curiosity.

'Sally Rose, you've just spent an hour closeted with an excruciatingly gorgeous man whose voice could melt brass and you tell me that nothing happened!'

'Well, it didn't. He was just checking out security. It's his job.'

Sally smiled reluctantly.

'He is rather gorgeous, isn't he?' she acknowledged.

'And what exactly did Mister All-American Hunk want?'

Sally ran a hand through her mop of dark, flyaway hair and sighed.

'Come on, Bella. Let's lock up and go and have a drink.'

Bella shook her head as she grabbed her coat and headed for the door, behind the last departing clients of the week.

'He must have spun you some incredible story to get you this rattled. Are you all right, love? You look kind of flushed.'

Flushed on the outside, pale on the inside, Sally thought as she turned on the alarm system, lowered the shutters and locked the door carefully behind them.

'I'm fine, just a bit tired. It's been quite a week. Did Rob phone?'

'No, but like you suggested if we didn't hear from him, I phoned him.

He said his foot was actually worse than he thought and he was going to have it X-rayed.'

'So, he won't be back Monday.'

Sally shivered and pulled her jacket closer around her. The sun had disappeared and there was an autumn chill in the air.

'We'd better get on to the theatrical agency as soon as possible. I can't handle this clown business as well as everything else. Besides, I'm no good at it.'

'I've already spoken with them.'

'And?'

'No joy, but I did tell Rob the problem and he said his brother's in town and wouldn't mind standing in for him for a while.'

'His brother? I didn't know he had a brother.'

'Well, apparently he has and he'll do the job for us. It'll be better than doing without. You know how well it works, bringing in the customers. The kids in the park expect it now. You can't disappoint them.'

'Why not? I've been disappointing them all this week. A clown who doesn't tumble and do crazy things is no fun.'

Bella patted her shoulder and shoved her gently through the door of the Edwardian pub where they usually unwound over a drink.

'You did the best you could,' Bella said, elbowing her way up to the bar, exchanging jolly riposte with some of the other locals as she squeezed her bulk between them. 'Same as usual, Meg. One large gin and tonic and one dry white wine for my slim friend here.'

They took their drinks to a window table and Sally tried not to look too worried. She had never been able to hide anything from Bella. Come to think of it, she had never wanted to hide anything from her. It wasn't fair of Gavin Calder to ask her not to talk about the situation. If he wanted to keep it secret, he shouldn't have involved her.

'Bella, I . . . '

Bella looked at her expectantly and she lowered her eyes and took another sip of wine.

'Look, I know I can trust you, Bella. There isn't anyone else I trust more.'

'But? Come on, Sal! What can you possibly have discussed with Mr Calder that's so high-powered and secret? He is a stranger, after all.'

Sally nodded. She almost gave way to the temptation to tell her cousin everything, but at the last moment she held back.

'I'm not sure what I'm getting into, Bella,' she said in a whisper so that the other customers in the bar couldn't hear. 'The thing is, I've agreed to help him, heaven knows why. I must be all kinds of fool. Anyway, if I tell you it could get you into trouble, too, if things go wrong.'

'I don't like the sound of this, Sal,' Bella said with a worried frown.

'You'll just have to trust me.'

'I trust you to land yourself into a

heap of trouble, that's what I trust you with.'

There was a sharp note of censure in Bella's voice.

'It's happened twice already, and this big American bloke looks like trouble to me.'

'I have every intention of being careful, Bella, but it's not what you think. I mean, it's nothing on a personal level and I've seen his credentials and they look pretty genuine.'

'Showed you a Mickey Mouse badge, did he? Oh, Sal! Why do you have to be so naive where good-looking men are concerned? Why don't you find yourself a nice, ordinary local lad? Goodness knows, there are plenty of them about who would jump at the chance of holding your hand in the back row of the cinema.'

Sally smiled at that.

'There has to be more than willingness on the part of any man to make him attractive to me,' she said and patted Bella's chubby hand as she got up to go. 'I'm whacked. See you on Monday.'

It was cold and starting to rain, but she walked slowly back to her flat, enjoying a few minutes of solitude to get her thoughts in order. She really did seem to be getting herself involved in a very sticky situation here. The American must have worked some kind of charm to get her to agree to his demands. The whole thing was crazy. When he came back on Monday she would tell him that she had changed her mind. He would have to find some other safe house to lodge his poor little rich girl.

The flat seemed particularly chilly and empty when she let herself in and switched on all the lights. She had got into the habit of lighting the place like Blackpool illuminations ever since they had had a break-in while she was watching the telly in the dark with a cup of cocoa in her hand. Sally shuddered and hurried to switch on the gas fire, sitting huddled over it until the place was warmed a bit.

Looking around her she felt she was seeing her home for the first time, seeing it through a stranger's eyes. It was pretty drab. Gavin Calder couldn't have thought much of the way she lived, not after the luxury he was probably used to. As soon as Rob got himself back to work, she promised herself, she would take some time off and redecorate. And maybe she would buy one or two bits of furniture that didn't look as if they came out of the local bric-a-brac shop.

It wasn't as if she couldn't afford to buy a few things to pretty up her lifestyle. She hadn't bothered because it hadn't seemed important. She had just been just so relieved to get out of a marriage that was too painful to support. Of course, when her aunt died, she could have had the house and what was in it, but she had never been happy with the old lady, so the house and its contents only served to remind her of her life there, her half-life. She had sold the house with its contents and bought The Rose Carousel, not that it was called that then.

It had been a paint and paper shop with a storeroom over it. It had taken a lot of time and hard work to turn it into her dream of a children's paradise and she was fiercely proud of the results. Now, it was time to take her own personal life into stock and think more in terms of a little more elegance, and a lot more comfort. After all, she hadn't been born a martyr, though her aunt would have liked to turn her into one.

Thinking again of Rob and his foot, her conscience pricked her and she decided to give him a ring and find out how he was. Maybe he needed her to do some shopping for him, cook him a meal or two. He had always been so good when she needed help. It was time to return the favour.

'Hello, Rob? It's me, Sally.'

But it wasn't Rob on the other end of the line. She heard a muffled, hasty conversation that sounded as if someone had put their hand over the mouthpiece. She wondered for a moment if Rob had got himself a new partner, since he had been without one for some time now. Then she remembered the brother.

There were one or two more noises as the handset was transferred and she recognised Rob's voice, though he sounded a bit strange.

'Hello, Sally. What are you phoning for? I mean . . . '

'Is it a bad time? I can hang up and you can ring me back if you like.'

'No, no, don't do that. It's all right. Did you want something?'

'Just to know how you were. How's the foot? Bella said it was worse.'

'The foot? Oh, yes. Well — um — yes, I — er — they think it's broken.'

'Have you had it X-rayed?'

'Tomorrow — er — yes, tomorrow. Sorry about the job, but . . . '

'Bella said your brother was going to help out.'

Sally hesitated as she could hear a constrained muttering in the background.

'I didn't know you had a brother, Rob.'

'No, well — er — we haven't seen each other in a long time. Family business, you know. It's all right now.'

'Is that who you've got with you now?'

'Who? Oh, yes. That's him. My brother.'

'What's his name?'

'His name?' There was a long pause, then he said quickly, 'Bruce. Look, sorry, Sally, but I have to go. I mean, there's somebody at the door.'

'Yes, all right. Tell Bruce I'll look forward to meeting him on Monday morning.'

She found herself speaking to an empty line, except for the purring in her ear that told her Rob had hung up without even saying goodbye. That wasn't like Rob. He was usually so well-mannered. She sighed and creased her forehead, hoping that Rob wasn't getting into another drinking session. He had been dry for two years now and seemed to be doing well.

Sally suddenly recalled her conversation with the American. He had made particular mention of Rob. He wasn't sure about him for some reason. She had to admit she didn't like the idea of either herself or her staff being checked up on by any security firm. Calder had a cheek to do this behind her back, treating them all like criminals under surveillance.

Sally got up and went to close the curtains. The nights were beginning to draw in and darkness was descending on the streets of Harrogate almost before the lamps were lit. Being a converted storeroom, there were windows both back and front, yet the world she could see from one side was very different from the other. At the front of the building the street was still active. The roads shone greasily and passing cars hissed along like snakes rushing for cover.

The back was a half-world of grey and black shadows that did not move. It was dead and silent with not even a cat to disturb a dustbin lid. It was a dark, sombre place, which was why Sally always liked to return home in relative daylight because the flat's private entrance was down there. It was something of a no-man's land and it scared her to be there even in daylight when the sun didn't shine.

She ate a simple cheese omelette and salad, listening to some Mozart, and then tried to settle down to read. At first, she couldn't concentrate. Her mind was far too busy to take in the printed words, so she ended up turning the pages blindly. Then her eyes closed and her head started nodding. At ten o'clock she decided she might as well go to bed and sleep off her exhaustion there. Tomorrow, she would rest and recuperate as much as possible before throwing herself into another busy week. It would get busier towards

Christmas. It always did. Toyshops were particularly hectic then.

Sally climbed into bed, jotted down a couple of ideas for a Christmas theme for the shop, then switched off her light and lay, strangely awake now, staring up at the invisible ceiling. She must have dropped off to sleep at some stage, because she awoke with a start, wondering what she had heard. There were often disturbing noises in the night. It was an old building. The timbers shifted and creaked, mice scratched and gnawed.

She opened her eyes and felt completely blind in the blanket of darkness that enveloped her. It was a moonless night and as silent as the grave. Two o'clock, her bedside alarm told her. She groaned and turned over, facing the window. She had opened the curtains after putting out the main light because she preferred to wake up naturally with the rising sun unless it was winter, then the alarm had to be set.

There it was again, a soft, rasping, grating sound. She sat up, propping herself on her elbows. It seemed to be coming from the yard down below. Sally slid out of bed and padded barefoot to the window, keeping well back out of sight as she peered out. She could see nothing.

She shrugged and started to turn away, but then a sudden light made her halt and started her heart off at a gallop. The flare of a match had lit up a face half turned away in shadow. Then she saw the red glow of a lit cigarette being drawn and a tell-tale wisp of grey smoke against the blackness.

How had he got in? There was a seven-foot wall all around the yard. But then, the intruder was exceptionally tall. The wall would not have presented much of a problem to him, especially if he was fit and athletic — like Gavin Calder.

Sally crossed the wide expanse of the apartment, not needing light to find what she was looking for. She triggered the alarm, then shot back to the window in time to see the intruder launch himself at the top of the wall and virtually throw himself over and back into the deserted road at the rear. A minute later she heard the soft, distant clunk of a car door and an engine starting up. It purred down the lane behind the children's garden area.

The two young constables who appeared in answer to the alarm summons, of course, thought she was behaving neurotically. After all, she was a young woman living alone and these things happen!

# 4

Monday was as dreary a day as it could be in the north of England at the beginning of September, and Sally felt as dull as dishwater as she opened up The Rose Carousel at eight o'clock. It was earlier than usual, but she had agreed to meet Gavin Calder at eight-fifteen.

He came on time, alone. She was glad on both counts since she had something to say to him and she didn't want any witnesses, especially a five-year-old who could hardly be expected to understand grown-up attitudes.

'Sally.'

He nodded as he came through the door, acknowledging her presence. Then he turned and locked the door behind him and she was left staring at the dark hair on the back of his head and the broad shoulders that filled out his jacket and tapered down to his narrowed hips.

'Thank you for being here.'

'Usually, when I say I'll do something, I do it,' Sally said and was treated to a disarming smile as he turned back to face her. 'However, on this occasion, I'm going to change my mind.'

His smile faded and the angry shadow that now replaced it made her wonder what it would be like to get on the wrong side of Mister Gavin Calder. Perhaps she was about to find out.

'What do you mean? I thought we had an arrangement.'

'I'm sorry, but I don't want to put myself on the line looking after your employer's daughter while you sort out a kidnapping threat.'

Sally's voice shook slightly.

'I'm a simple shopkeeper, Mr Calder, not a C I A agent.'

'I didn't think you were the type of person to go back on your promises, Ms Rose, especially where a five-year-old child is concerned.'

51

He approached her and she automatically backed away until the small of her back was pressed against the counter behind which she normally spent most of her working day.

'This has nothing to do with Anna. I've had time to think things over and I don't think I'm the right person to oblige you, Mr Calder.'

'Oh, I don't know about that. It depends what you mean by obliging me, doesn't it?'

'I'm not going to parry words with you, Gavin.'

'Ah! We're back on first-name terms. That's a good sign.'

'Dream on, Mister Big Shot! You don't intimidate me one iota!'

If only, Sally thought, he knew just how intimidated she felt at that moment!

'I wasn't thinking of intimidating you, Sally. I just want to save Anna. She's been through too much already for such a small person. You seem to have a way with children. I heard it from various independent sources and I've seen it with my own eyes. Yes! I've been watching you for some time and not all the time when you were dressed as a clown and sussed me out in the park. You're good, Sally. You're a very kind, loving young woman. I feel I could trust my own daughter in your keeping.'

'What would your important employer say?'

'I speak for my employer.'

'Who is he?'

'That doesn't have to concern you.'

'Oh, but it does! It concerns me very much. You come here looking like some left-over from the Mafia and tell me that you're protecting a child from being kidnapped. You want to use my business as a hideaway.'

'I prefer to think of it as a safe house.'

'Whatever! How do I know you're not the kidnapper? Eh? Can you tell me that?'

'No, I can't tell you that. You'll just have to trust me.'

'How can I trust a man who stands in my backyard in the middle of the night smoking a cigarette as if he's part of a lonely smokers' campaign?'

'I don't smoke, Sally.'

'I told the police about you.'

'It wasn't me in your backyard. What did you tell them?'

'Only that there was an intruder at two this morning and that he was tall and smoked. Dammit, I saw you!'

'One of your admirers perhaps.'

'I don't have . . . '

She skidded to a halt. No point in letting this man know that she did not have any admirers, not that he would care.

He stepped forward and she could feel the material of his suit touching her through the fine wool of her dress, feel the heat of him, smell the heady aftershave. He gripped her upper arms and put his face down to hers and suddenly he didn't seem so tall and she hated herself for enjoying the close proximity of this man who frightened her.

'Don't!' she warned and a slow smile crept across his face, lighting up his eyes.

'You don't for one minute think I'm planning to kiss you, do you?' he asked and she stiffened in his hold. 'I don't get what I want by that means, Sally. I only take what I want when the other party is willing, and able.'

It was an insult to her femininity and suddenly she kicked out at his shin and as he jerked away with the pain of the blow, she pulled back her hand and brought it sharply across his face. The resounding slap made him blink, but she couldn't help feeling that it had hurt her more than it had done him any damage. His head tilted to one side in a lop-sided nod and she heard a deep-throated chuckle.

'That was quite impressive, Sally,' he said. 'I'd say that in a tight spot you could take care of yourself quite adequately.'

'It has been known,' she told him, surreptitiously hiding her stinging palm in a clenched fist behind her back.

'I see. What a pity. Kissing can be a lot of fun.'

'That depends on who's doing it to whom.'

'Who hurt you, Sally?' he asked. 'It must have been pretty bad to render you so frigid.'

Sally stuck her hands on her hips and her eyes came out on stalks.

'I am not frigid. You men! You are so conceited. Just because you're handsome you think every woman's going to grovel at your feet. Well, it's not true.'

'Thank you for handsome, however, where I come from women tend to go for the plain, dependable types. Me, I get stuck with gold-digging harpies who think I'm a stepping-stone to fame and fortune. Don't talk to me about being used, ma'am!'

Then they were standing there just looking at one another and reading the signals that passed between them like silent vibrations. Eventually, Sally shrugged.

'It seems like we've both had a taste of the bittersweet. So, who hurt you, Gavin?'

'Another time, Sally. Right now, I . . .'

Their conversation was interrupted by a rattle at the front door and they turned to see a small face pressed up against the glass. Two chubby hands were raised, gripping the handle and working it up and down. The wide, spaniel-brown eyes moved from Gavin to Sally and back again to Gavin, filled with pleading.

'What on earth? That blasted nanny!' he exploded.

Gavin projected himself across the floor of the shop and pulled back the bolt. The child almost fell inside and clutched him around his knees.

'Anna, what are you doing? Where's Lorraine? I told her to wait in the car with you.'

The child didn't respond other than

fixing him with large, tearful eyes. Such a lovely child, Sally thought, and she had to contend with a nanny and this goon to look after her. It was criminal.

'Hello, Anna!'

Sally stepped forward and touched the child gently on her pale cheek. Anna looked up at her, blinking furiously to keep the tears at bay.

'You remember me, don't you? I'm Sally Rose and I own The Rose Carousel. I remember the last time you were here. You liked this toy carousel, didn't you? Look, Anna. It plays pretty music if you wind this little key at the bottom.'

She turned the key a few times and the small carousel started to turn, its tiny white alabaster horses going up and down to the music.

'Do you recognise the music, Anna? It's from Oliver Twist. I'm sure you've seen the film.'

Sally sang along to the tune, but then got all choked up on the words of Where Is Love? Anna took the music box and turned it over delicately in her small hands. She looked up at Sally with a radiant smile that transformed her unhappy face.

'You can keep that, sweetheart. My present to you.'

She glanced over at Gavin and found his eyes on her. They seemed to have lost a lot of their hardness.

'She's beautiful. Who on earth would want to . . . '

Gavin frowned and she fell silent, as silent as the child beside her who was now slipping a hand into hers.

'I'd say you've just made a great big hit,' Gavin said gruffly. 'And it's nothing to do with the giving of much-coveted gifts. Anna might come from a rich background, but it takes more than money to make a child happy.'

Sally returned her attention to Anna.

'I bet you'd like a ride on the big carousel, wouldn't you?'

The child's eyes widened and she nodded, her small head bobbing, disturbing the dark curls that framed her pretty face. While Sally went to switch on the mechanism that worked the carousel and the lights and the hurdy-gurdy music, she noticed that Anna had returned to Gavin and was gripping his hand as if it was something she had done naturally all her life. This wasn't a child afraid of her minder, she decided. The child loved the big American. It was mirrored in her eyes every time she looked at him.

Not only that — Gavin reciprocated the emotion. Oh, he tried to hide it all right, but it was there. Sally was no fool when it came to love. Her own childhood had been too lacking in it for her not to recognise it now.

The bigger version of the carousel was now in motion, its great white stallions slowly rising and lowering themselves. Gavin picked up Anna and slung her astride the one she pointed to, the one with the unicorn's head and the golden crown.

'Hang on tight, Anna!' he instructed

her, then mounted the horse behind.

The speed of the carousel picked up as the lights flashed through all the colours of the spectrum. Anna squealed and laughed, thoroughly enjoying herself . . . Gavin, too.

It was during the third undulating circuit that Gavin suddenly bent low from the waist and Sally, who had been standing close to the rostrum, found herself being swept up into his strong arms and placed before him between the saddle and his horse's neck. She cried out in surprise, then laughed with man and child at the sheer madness of the whole scene.

When the music finally petered out and the carousel came to rest, Sally, embarrassed to have been clasped so tightly against Gavin during the ride, slithered off and quickly adjusted her dress which had rucked up around her hips. Gavin helped Anna to the floor, then turned to her.

'There's still a child in all of us, Sally,' he said softly, tipping her chin up with his thumb and forefinger. 'You just have to let it out occasionally.'

Then he kissed her. She couldn't believe that she stood there and let a perfect stranger kiss her in the middle of the shop floor. OK, so he wasn't such a complete stranger any more and the shop was empty, so who was there to complain — except her? But Sally didn't feel like complaining. She wanted him to do it again, so she could kiss him back.

'All right?' Gavin asked, putting a steadying hand on her shoulder.

She blinked at him, feeling her head spin.

'Yes. Just a bit dizzy. It'll pass in a moment. I'm not used to all that centrifugal force.'

His mouth twisted into a wry smile.

'I'm glad about that. I'd hate my kiss to be responsible for you losing your head.'

'Hm,' was all she could say, then, with a hand to her head to tidy her mussed hair, she saw that the staff was beginning to arrive and she was painfully aware that she was blushing.

'Well, what did you think of that, Anna?'

She bent down low to the little girl so her embarrassment was hidden from all.

'Anna can't speak,' she heard Gavin remind her from above her head and looked up at him sharply, the unspoken question plain in her eyes. 'She hasn't spoken since she was three, but we're working on it, aren't we, Anna?'

Gavin's words seemed to stick in his throat. He kneeled down and took the child in his arms. She clung to his neck and kissed him loudly on the cheek.

'You stay with Sally, sweetheart,' he told her in a half-whisper, his face nuzzled into her neck. 'She'll look after you while I'm out working. You understand, don't you, Anna?'

Anna nodded gravely and he stood up and laid a hand on Sally's shoulder.

'You will, won't you? Look after her for me?'

Sally nodded dumbly and watched him stride away, brushing past Bella in the doorway.

'You didn't tell him to get lost!'

Bella was quick to come to Sally's side and hissed in Sally's ear.

'Idiot!'

'Perhaps,' Sally croaked, then looked down at the child whose hand had found its way into hers again. 'Come on, Anna. We've got real, live animals in the garden. I bet you'd like to help me feed them.

# 5

Gavin Calder, having called back later in the day to check that all was well, was watching his small charge closely as she played happily with the other children, riding on the carousel whenever the opportunity presented itself.

'She seems to be settling down well,' he said happily.

'She's fine,' Sally told him. 'When will you call for her? We close normally at six o'clock. Eight on Fridays and Saturdays to allow time for working parents to visit.'

Gavin seemed to be studying the question as if it posed some kind of deep problem. Then he swept over her with his dark, mysterious eyes and she winced. It was almost as if he could read her mind, see beyond the brittle, outer veneer she had built around herself in the past few years.

'I can't guarantee anything at this stage. I've explained it all to Anna and I think she understands.'

'That's all very well for Anna, but what about me? I don't seem to be following you at all. What time will you be collecting her?'

'I can't give you precise times. Hold on to her until I contact you, or until I turn up. Don't, whatever you do, hand her over to anyone other than me. Is that clear, Sally?'

'It's very clear.'

'Right. I'll leave you now so the two of you can get better acquainted. I presume your staff have been told to keep a very tight guard on the child.'

'I haven't had the opportunity yet to speak to them, but I will soon. They're pretty reliable, I can assure you.'

'Very well. What will you tell them?'

'That she's my niece.'

Sally wrinkled her nose as she spoke, reminding herself how she hated lies of any kind.

'That she's having family problems

and needs looking after because she's unpredictable and may try to run away. OK?'

'OK.' Then his face dimpled into a smile. 'Are you sure you were never in the secret services?'

'Excuse me, Mr Calder,' she said, ignoring his remark and brushed past him with a smile to match his own. 'I think I see my new member of staff arriving.'

Gavin glanced up and studied the man entering the shop with a nervous, almost furtive expression on his long, dour face.

'Name?' he asked Sally.

'The same as Rob's, I assume. Barlow — Bruce Barlow. It's Rob's brother. He's going to help us out while Rob is indisposed.'

Gavin rubbed at his chin thought-fully. As Sally approached the newcomer, extending a hand and a bright word of welcome, the big American slipped silently out behind him, with only the very briefest of glances in Anna's direction.

'Hi, there!' Sally said to the man, who was probably in his mid-thirties, tall, athletic looking and swarthy, with a two-day beard that only just looked like it might be part of the fashion of the day. 'I'm Sally Rose. You must be Bruce.'

He looked about him uncertainly, narrowing his eyes as they swept over the group of pre-school children that were clambering on the carousel. Sally knew it was wrong to make instant judgements, but she was sure she was not going to like the man.

'You don't look anything like Rob.'

Bruce Barlow's chin lifted and he fixed her with colourless eyes that didn't quite go with the thinning, dark hair on his bony head. Rob was sandy fair, sandy with bright blue eyes and delicate features. This man had a Neanderthal streak half a mile long. She half expected him to grunt a response.

'We're only half brothers,' he said

and she couldn't place the accent.

It seemed to have a mingling of many regional burrs all blended together, but was more southern than northern. Rob was a Scot.

'Well, if you'd like to come into the staff restroom, Bruce, I'll explain the job and show you where things are.'

At that moment, Anna broke away from her new friends of the day and came to install herself at Sally's side.

'Who's she? Your daughter?' Bruce asked, but paid no more than a moment's attention to Anna.

'This is Anna, my niece,' Sally said, surprised at how easy the lies came, once you started the ball rolling. 'She's staying with us for a while.'

Bruce gave her a sceptical look, then proceeded to ignore Anna.

'I don't have any papers. They're sending them on.'

'That's all right.'

Sally smiled. Dammit! I don't like him! Catching sight of her cousin entering the shop, late back from lunch and breathless, as usual, she called her over.

'Bella! Excuse me, Bruce, but my assistant, Bella, is by far the best person to show you the ropes. Bella, this is Rob's brother. He's come to help us out. Show him what to do, will you?'

Bella's eyes widened and then her astute green eyes travelled up and down the new man without registering too much pleasure. They would compare notes later, but Sally thought she and Bella would agree on what they saw, even at first glance.

'OK! Come with me, Bruce. Tell me, how long do you think Rob's going to be on sick leave? He's sorely missed around here.'

Sally watched Bella drag Bruce off towards the staffroom. Bella was a big woman. If she was determined that you should go some place, you didn't argue. Bruce was no different to anybody else. He went with her, as meek and mild as a lamb to the slaughter.

'What is it, Anna? Did you want something?'

Sally looked down at the little girl who was tugging at her hand. Anna nodded, then shook her head and frowned. It struck Sally that the child was having difficulty coping with her lack of verbal communication.

'I don't know what you want, sweetie, but I tell you what. We can communicate if you write it down. OK? You can write, can't you?'

Anna nodded enthusiastically. Sally found a board and a crayon.

**Where is he?**

Anna wrote the words slowly and laboriously. Sally took the crayon from her and wrote, **Who?** Anna wrote, **Daddy.** Then she rubbed it out and hastily scribbled the word, **Gavin.**

'I don't know where he is at the moment, Anna,' Sally told the child gently. 'He has work to do. He's asked me to look after you for a while.'

Anna nodded, but her face was sad.

'You like Gavin, don't you?' Sally asked the child.

Anna's face lit up. She nodded.

'Well, when you like someone, when it feels good in here . . . ' Sally indicated her midriff ' . . . you have to trust them. Do you understand the word trust, Anna?'

Another nod. Suddenly she pointed to the staffroom door and shook her head while pulling a long face.

'Bella?' Sally asked tentatively, but the response was negative. 'Bruce? The new man?'

Affirmative.

'You don't like him?' Sally asked and Anna answered with another shake of the head.

'Me neither, Anna. He's not our type of person, but he's helping us out while Rob is nursing his broken foot. You would like Rob. He's very funny and very gentle. All the children like him.'

As soon as Bruce donned the clown's outfit, just managing to get into Rob's costume, Sally saw a complete transformation and relaxed somewhat. He became JoJo on the instant. He effected a high, clown-like voice, laughed and joked with children and parents alike, even bringing a smile to the most serious face.

A few days later, it was as if he had been doing the job for years. Sally still didn't like the man, but she couldn't fault his work and she was grateful not to have to be the stand-in clown any longer.

'Well, I didn't think I'd say this, but the man is good,' Bella nodded in Bruce's direction where he was playing the fool around the carousel, climbing up on the horses, balancing, cartwheeling and doing hand-stands, to great applause.

'Exactly what I was thinking,' Sally nodded slowly, her eyes searching out Anna. 'Even Anna is warming to him and she didn't like him at all at first.'

'That kid has good taste for one so young.'

Bella gave a low laugh and returned Anna's joyful wave as she whirled around and up and down on her favourite unicorn.

'Just look at her. I'd say she was born in the saddle.'

'Well, they are Americans, Bella, and rich. They probably have horses in their blood.'

'And what, do you think, does your Mister Wonderful have in his blood, eh?'

Bella gave Sally a wicked wink.

'Iced water, probably,' Sally said grumpily, though she wasn't at all sure that she believed that.

Gavin was an unusually attractive man and, of course, it was that foreignness about him that appealed to her, the dark, good-looking face that had a toughness about it, marked with a life that had not been easy all the way, and the eyes that seemed to be able to see right down inside her. But it was his smile that really turned her knees to water and made her heart palpitate, not that she would admit that to Bella.

Much as she loved her cousin, she knew that if she told her this tiny secret, she would be plagued for ever more on the subject of Gavin Calder, and whichever way she looked at the situation, she knew it was only a temporary thing. Once he got the business of the kidnapping threats under control it would be over and she would probably never see him again.

By six o'clock, Gavin had not appeared to collect Anna, as usual. By seven, Anna was a little fractious and Sally was worried. Bella, sensing her anxiety, stayed behind, helping to amuse the small girl whom she had taken to her big, generous heart. In fact, there wasn't a member of staff at The Rose Carousel who hadn't taken to Anna in a big way. She was an adorable child.

'Don't worry, Anna,' Sally said as she stroked the little girl's velvety soft cheek and looked into the big, pleading eyes that were turned up to hers. 'Gavin is late, I know, but he'll come and get you eventually. Doesn't he always?'

A solemn nod.

'The kid's crazy about that man,' Bella commented with a shake of her head.

'Substitution,' Sally murmured, her chin on her hand.

They had closed up the shop and gone up to the flat, which was the arrangement she had made with Gavin in the event of him not turning up before closing time. Sally was tired and she had a mammoth headache that didn't want to go away, despite numerous doses of aspirin, which she only ever took in an emergency. It had been a long, hard day and even Anna was beginning to look tired and bored.

'Look, Sal, why don't you grab a breath of fresh air?' Bella suggested. 'I'll stay here with Anna. You'll be all right with me, sweetie, won't you?'

Anna looked uncertain and Sally knew why. Gavin had schooled the child well on what she could or could not do in his absence. She was very fond of Bella naturally, but she had been told to stay with Sally at all times and she was a surprisingly obedient little girl.

'No, I think we'd better wait here,' Sally replied.

But Anna was tugging at her hand, dragging her to the door. Her eyes had lit up at the mention of going out for a walk and Sally couldn't really see the danger in a short stroll down to the park and back.

'All right, Anna. We'll go for a short walk, eh? That is if Bella will hold the fort till we get back.'

Bella rolled her eyes to the ceiling.

'Silly question,' she said with a sucking sound to her teeth that sounded like Sally's great-aunt Jane. 'Go on with you. If Gavin comes I'll just have to entertain him with my beauty and wit.'

'Don't try too hard. You might frighten him off!'

'Gee, honey, it's great having you for a friend!' Bella affected a bad American accent, then gave a giggle. 'Oh, go on, Sal. What harm can it do? It strikes me both you and Anna are badly in need of a breath of air.'

Anna was nodding enthusiastically. Sally looked at her and thought about it for a while, then told the child to fetch their coats.

'All right, Bella,' she said. 'We won't be long and, with a bit of luck, we'll be back before Gavin shows, if he shows at all.'

'If he shows? What do we do with Anna if he doesn't? Do you have their address or what?'

'No, but . . . '

Sally flapped her hands in frustration and heaved a sigh.

'Oh, Bella, don't look at me like that!'

'Like what?'

'Like I'm some kind of naive fool. You know, the kind who buys things with a credit card without realising she has to pay the bill at the end of the month.'

'Would I ever? You don't know how to contact him, do you?'

'No.'

Bella's head immediately sank to the side and she pulled in her mouth to show her disapproval.

'Just what is the story, Sal? Do you really know what you're doing?'

'I can't tell you anything, Bella. It's a question of security, and I'm responsible, or partly responsible, for Anna's safety.'

Bella started to say something, but then Anna came back with the coats looking radiant at the thought of going out.

'Don't worry. He'll be here soon,' Sally told her as they left through the shop and she locked the door behind them.

It was a beautiful evening after an unusually warm, sunny day. The sun was setting slowly, igniting the remaining clouds with patches of turquoise blue. The trees in the park were etched with gold.

'Oh, Anna! Isn't this super?'

Sally looked down at the tiny, heart-shaped face and didn't need words to tell her that Anna was enjoying the outing, too.

'Ouch! Sorry, stone in my shoe. Let's sit down for a minute.'

They headed for a park bench and sat down. Sally removed her trainer, shook out the offending stone, which had felt like a huge rock, but was more like a grain of sand. She replaced the shoe and leaned back, eyes closed, soaking in the freshness all around her.

Maybe she actually dozed, just for an instant. She wasn't sure, but suddenly, she heard a shout and recognised Gavin's voice. There was a screech of tyres. When she opened her eyes, Anna was no longer sitting by her side. Sally jumped to her feet and searched the area all around where she had been sitting, but Anna was not there. Still, she had definitely heard Gavin's voice, unless it had been some kind of dream.

Then she saw them, security officer and child. He had Anna in his arms and he was standing just outside the park gates. When he saw her hurrying towards him his face registered the utmost anger and she shrivelled inside.

'What on earth were you thinking of?'

Gavin's voice was a hiss of anger and his eyes seemed to throw spears into the very heart of her being.

'I'm sorry, but one minute she was there and the next . . . '

'You were supposed to be looking after her! What were you doing, woman?'

Anna started to cry and Gavin tried clumsily to comfort her, but his anger was too great to allow any softness to come through.

'You were so late and we were both tired of playing games.'

Sally tried hard to keep her voice steady, but she was shaking too much.

'We just came out for a stroll and a

breath of fresh air. What's wrong with that?'

Gavin fixed her with a malevolent stare.

'What's wrong with that? I just caught Anna before she was dragged into a passing car, that's what's wrong with that! I'm going to have to re-think some on this arrangement we have. You're obviously not the right person to take care of Anna.'

'Don't you dare speak to me like that, Gavin Calder!' Sally raged, not thinking of anything but the loss of Anna in her life.

The child had become rather special to her. The thought of losing her so soon was hard to take. And in losing Anna, Sally knew she would also lose Gavin, not that she had ever had him. Even in her dreams he had seemed too far away to reach, on another level, another world.

# 6

Gavin had taken Anna away, refusing to listen to any arguments. After telling Sally, in no uncertain terms, that she had fallen down sadly on her side of the arrangement, he had stormed off without a backward glance.

Anna had cried bitterly, reaching out over his shoulder to Sally. She obviously did not like Gavin's decision and was objecting strongly, the only way she knew how, against being taken away from her new-found friend.

'Cheer up, love.'

Bella came and gave Sally a tight hug, which didn't really help and made her want to cry.

'Come on. Forget the big lout and his precious little cargo. Let's go and treat ourselves to a fish and chip supper, eh? It's the least you owe me after keeping me back so late. Come on, I won't take no for an answer. Haddock and double chips with mushy peas and bread and butter.'

'I thought you were on a diet!'

Bella looked desolate.

'All this business with you and Gavin and Anna is making me anxious. I have to eat, otherwise I'll suffer a breakdown of morale and that's not a pretty sight. How about it, eh?'

'Oh, all right. Why not? After all, it's not every day I'm told I'm not fit to look after a small child by an American thug who probably wouldn't know what to do with a child if one hit him in the face.'

'That's something of a complex riddle and I'm not up to it at this time of night.'

Bella shrugged herself into her coat and marched Sally to the door.

'You're better out of it, Sal, believe me. A man like that! Why, anybody can see how easily he could tie a person's hormones in knots.'

Sally could feel laughter bubbling up

through her suppressed tears. She knew exactly what her cousin meant. The trouble was, her hormones had been knotted ever since she first laid eyes on Gavin Calder. And now he had walked out of her life as suddenly as he had walked into it, and she hadn't even had time to get to know him properly.

Oh, the shame of it, the waste. There was something sinful about him, something dangerous. As a whole, it came over as more than just a little exciting. If he had crooked his little finger, she would have gone running towards him, no questions asked. It was as bad as that. What a fool she must be! What an absolute, utter fool, to think that this man was worthy of any feelings approaching love.

No, not love. How could you love somebody you hardly knew? No. If it was anything, it had to be lust. Whatever it was, it was the first time it had happened to her to such a profoundly disturbing degree.

The fish and chips were good. By the

time Sally got back home to the flat, she was beginning to feel better. There was no point, she kept telling herself, in moping about the place, dreaming of things that might have happened. They didn't happen, and, she thought, let's face it, they probably would never have happened anyway.

She put on some restful music and sipped a large gin and tonic, which was more in Bella's line, but good for zapping temporary despair. She would not brood over Anna and her dark, grizzly keeper. Let Gavin sort things out in his own way. According to him, he had done it all before. It must be really hard-working for a rich man who expected miracles at every turn, but even worse to be a rich man's daughter and have to put up with things such as kidnapping and the trauma that goes with it. Poor Anna probably saw very little of her father, so it was fortunate she had a caring protector in Gavin Calder.

During the next few days, Sally tried

to block Gavin and Anna from her thoughts, push the whole incident to the back of her memory. It wasn't easy. In fact, it was incredibly hard, bordering on the impossible. All the time, there was this gnawing in her stomach, the biting desire to see him again and to have Anna's baby-soft hand nestling in hers once more.

If I had a daughter, Sally thought, I'd like her to be just like Anna. How difficult it must be for her — a mother who walked out, a father who didn't care just as long as he didn't have to pay out any more ransom money and . . . The door rattled sharply, making Sally look up from her gloomy meanderings. It was Saturday and she had just locked up for the day. As usual, it had been a hectic day in the shop and already she was preparing for the Christmas onslaught.

'Sally!'

She eased the door blind aside and saw a familiar silhouette etched by the street lamp outside. Switching on the main shop lights, she pulled back the double lock, switched off the security system and opened the door to Gavin Calder.

'I hoped I'd catch you before you stopped for the night.'

His dark eyes looked even darker and more daunting than ever.

'I don't see why,' she told him caustically. 'I had the idea that any business between us was terminated, Mr Calder. Let's just leave it at that, shall we?'

There was a short silence between them, then his expression softened and his hand somehow found hers and held on to it tightly.

'Don't you want to know how Anna is?' he asked and she felt her heart start to spin.

'Why should I? You've already told me that I'm useless at looking after her. That usually goes with a non-caring attitude, does it not?'

He rubbed a hand over his face. He looked tired and worried, but there was something else in his expression that she couldn't fathom out.

'I didn't actually say that and I certainly don't believe it,' he said quietly. 'I've come to apologise for my behaviour, Sally. It was just a spur-of-the-moment thing when I was concerned for Sally's safety. I saw someone try to drag her into a car. What I didn't see was you supervising her, as you were supposed to be.'

'It had been an awful day, Gavin. My replacement clown had called in sick in the afternoon and I was back playing JoJo in the park. When I took Anna out later, I closed my eyes for one second. She slipped away. I don't know why and I don't much care. Children do things like that when parents least expect them to.'

'And so many children are abducted, violated, tortured and murdered, just because they managed to slip out of that careless parental ring of authority.'

'That doesn't mean that the parents don't care what happens to little Jean or Johnnie. Nobody's perfect every minute of the day, Gavin. Not even you!'

He inclined his head.

'I admit that children are a sight more difficult to keep an eye on than adults, and I've come to apologise for my behaviour the other night. You're not the only one who has long, hard days. I'd had a humdinger, too. Seeing Anna about to be abducted was the last straw.'

'Is that all, Mr Calder, or are you going to keep me standing here all night?'

He blinked at that.

'I'm sorry. I didn't mean to. Look, Sally . . . '

'Yes?'

'Can we talk, in your flat? It's a little public here in the doorway.'

Sally hesitated. Did she really want to have any more to do with this man? Ever since they met, he had taken her for granted while he acted the big, handsome hero, making her feel vulnerable and inadequate all at the same time.

'I really don't think we have anything more to say, do you?'

'Perhaps you're right, but I'm not thinking right now of you or of myself, but of Anna. She's very unhappy, Sally. I have my hands full. I can't cope with her.'

'Then tell your rich boss to hire an army of nannies.'

'You don't understand.'

'That's right. I don't understand why a five-year-old child should be neglected and turned over into the hands of a security man just because her parents are too busy to care about what happens to her. They are the people who should be looking after Anna, not you, not me. If I had a child like that . . . '

'You'd be a wonderful mother. That's obvious, Sally.'

Sally gulped at his words. She had been expecting another dressing down, but instead, he was standing there delivering compliments, and she liked it!

'I certainly wouldn't be handing her over to strangers to look after,' she said sharply. 'The poor little mite mustn't know who she is half the time. How much time does she spend with her father anyway? Does she ever hear from her mother?'

'You ask too many questions, Sally.'

Gavin looked off into the middle distance, avoiding her questioning eyes.

'As I've already said, there are things I can't tell you. I can only ask you to have confidence in me.'

'What's the point? The deal is off. I don't want the responsibility. If Anna's own father and his security force can't look after the child, it's a pathetic situation.'

'Yes, I'm inclined to agree with you, for the record, that is, and I was all set to find somebody else after that happened. I realise now that I panicked.'

'Tough security men aren't supposed to panic.'

'That may be so, but if anything happened to Anna, I'd never forgive myself.'

'Or anyone else, it seems to me.'

Sally met his cool gaze and held it.

'OK, Gavin. Maybe I deserved having a strip torn off me for not being observant enough, but it was a brief moment's lapse of concentration because I was too weary to think. I do have a business to run, you know, staff to control, problems to sort out. A little girl that's as silent and as fast as quicksilver is a bit of a challenge for someone largely inexperienced with the more intimate side of looking after young children. I love Anna. She's beautiful and adorable and surprisingly unspoiled. However, I definitely do not want you to ask me to continue looking after her for you.'

'I'm not the one doing the asking, Sally.'

'What?'

'It's Anna herself who wants to come back here. She's been miserable and depressed ever since — well, ever since I took her away. I can do nothing with her.'

'I'm sorry, but I can't help. Couldn't you contact her mother or someone?'

'Her mother is the last person I want to contact.'

Gavin had placed himself firmly before her and now he was holding her by the shoulders, the heat of his hands penetrating the fine angora of her sweater.

'Sally, I apologise for my behaviour. It was wrong of me to fly off the handle like that, but, as I said, I panicked, seeing her being hauled into that car. I blame you, even though I knew that I was at fault. If I'd come back on time, it would never have happened and you wouldn't have been so tired you didn't notice her slip away.'

'And why didn't you come back on time, Gavin?' Sally couldn't help asking the question that had been nagging her.

'It couldn't be that your private life got in the way of the job at hand, could it?'

'Sally!'

He gave her a little shake and pulled her even closer, so that they were almost touching.

'I am perfectly capable of doing my job and keeping my private life separate. And right now my private life could do with a little relaxation, preferably with the right person.'

She didn't expect the kiss and when it came, so suddenly and with more than a little passion behind its force, every bone in her body seemed to melt. She should have been rigid, angry, fighting against him, but she could only manage the tiniest show of reluctance before she fell willingly into his arms.

'That was unfair!' she croaked when his head finally came up and he gasped for air.

'What was unfair about it?' he wanted to know and she could still feel his heart tapping against her chest, matching hers beat for beat. 'I've wanted to do that since the day we met and you know it.'

'No! You're just taking advantage of me, trying to get round me, because you're desperate to palm Anna off on to somebody, anybody.'

'That's not true, Sally.'

'Then what is the truth, Gavin?'

'The truth is that Anna is a five-year-old child who is frightened and confused, traumatised by what's happened in the past and hungry for love. I'm doing my very best to remove the element of danger from her life. While I'm doing that I can't give her the attention, the affection, she craves. She adores you, Sally. You can fill the void in her life right now. If you say no, I don't know how I'm going to face her when she finds out that her best friend, Sal, doesn't want her either.'

'Oh, stop it! Stop it! You're just playing on my sympathies and I hate you for it.'

'You don't really hate me, Sally.'

Gavin turned her back to him and tightened his hold again. She felt her small world tipping. It made her strangely giddy.

'I do.'

'No, you don't. Those eyes of yours don't lie, even if your lips do. You can tell me a million times that you hate me, but I only have to look into your eyes to see that hate is far from what you're feeling right now.'

'Damn you! Are you always right?'

'Most of the time, yes. Don't turn your head away.'

Gavin now released her and placed his hands on either side of her face, tilting her head up so that he could read her expression more clearly.

'Why are you so afraid of loving somebody, Sally? Those two guys in your earlier life must have really made a mess of your emotions.'

'Who said anything about love?'

Sally tried to jerk her head away, but

he held her fast and, besides, she didn't really want him to let go.

'Attraction, lust, sex, call it what you will at the moment,' he said while he was giving her face tiny, tantalising butterfly kisses that were sending her body crazy with desire. 'That's how it all starts out. With some people it never goes beyond that. Believe me, I know.'

'Is there anything you don't know?'

'Uh-huh!'

His mouth had found hers again. She quivered ecstatically, shuddering against him, feeling the muscles in his tightly-tuned torso ripple in response.

'What?' she asked breathlessly.

'I don't know how long I'm going to be able to hold off before I really want you.'

The sound of his mobile phone beeping shrilly at that precise point in time made them both jump apart and stand there blinking at one another. For a few wonderful moments they had both been lost in a mass of unexplored emotions, anxious to explore. Now, the bubble had burst.

'Blast!'

Gavin pulled out the phone and spoke quickly into it.

'Yeah, yeah! OK. I'll get right on to it. Yeah, 'bye.'

'Work?' Sally said, not sure whether she was glad or angry at the interruption. Everything had been going ahead too fast for comfort, like freewheeling downhill without brakes.

'Work? We've just drawn a lead on the possible kidnapper. I have to get back on the job.'

'I see.'

Of course, she understood, but she couldn't hide her disappointment. He wanted her and she had never wanted any man quite the way she wanted Gavin Calder. Gavin reached out and touched her flushed cheek.

'I'll bring Anna back just as soon as I'm able. OK?'

Sally bit down on her lip.

'Yes, of course,' she said, wondering

why she should feel such a warning churn in her stomach.

There was something not quite right with all this, but she had no idea how she could get to the bottom of it.

# 7

Sally roamed restlessly about the flat after Gavin left. There were too many raw emotions running riot inside her to allow her to remain in one place for more than a few seconds at a time, and all her emotions were conflicting ones.

On the one hand, she had this growing attraction for the big American. Actually, it was more of an obsession. She couldn't get him out of her mind and the body she thought would never feel anything again for any man was betraying her badly. On the other hand, she couldn't help wondering if he wasn't just playing her for a sucker because he needed somebody to make his job of looking after Anna easier.

And, of course, there was Anna herself. Sally had taken all of five minutes to decide that this was her idea of the ideal child. Looking after her had not been the real pain. It had been the overwork caused first by Rob's non-return to work and then his brother's sudden illness. Sally had been obliged to don, yet again, the outfit of JoJo the Clown.

She could have asked someone else, of course. She could, as the owner of The Rose Carousel, have insisted that someone take on the rôle, but she knew that nobody was keen on the idea, no more keen than she was. So, it was her responsibility, or lose a lot of business when she could ill afford to do so.

The money she had borrowed to extend into the land at the rear of the premises, in order to build a children's garden, play area and home farm, had to be repaid. That could only be done if she could keep on attracting large numbers of customers to the shop and tea-room.

Bella had offered to give JoJo a go, but the minute she put on the clown's suit, she had an acute attack of nerves.

She was full of apologies, but it was obvious that she couldn't possibly take on the rôle.

'Oh, why did he have to go and do that?' Sally moaned aloud, thinking of Gavin's kiss and the embrace that she had enjoyed a little too much. 'I was perfectly happy the way I was before he walked through that door.'

Sally pronounced a silent curse under her breath, flung herself down on her sofa and switched on the television. She wasn't an avid television fan, but she thought that perhaps it might take her mind off all that was happening in her life right now. She was wrong. The picture that flashed before her astonished eyes was that of Anna and the ticker-tape message that flowed beneath the picture spoke of a kidnapping that had been kept quiet by the girl's parents. Sally boosted the sound as the newsreader came into focus.

'American multi-millionaire, Lorn Macey, was not available today to talk to reporters, but his estranged wife has finally admitted that their daughter, Anna, five years old, was recently abducted. The family had been keeping the crime from the police and the Press in case of reprisals, but since no ransom has been demanded they are now concerned that this is not so much a kidnapping, but a possible case of murder. Chief suspect is security chief, Gavin Calder.'

A blurred but unmistakable photograph of Gavin flashed on to the screen.

'Gavin Calder, thirty-nine years of age and an ex-F B I agent with special responsibilities to the White House under the President, has not been seen or heard of since Anna's disappearance six weeks ago.'

Sally zapped off the television and sat there, oozing the cold perspiration of fear. She had fallen in love with — been taken for a ride by — a kidnapper! How could she have been taken in like that? He had seemed so normal and so nice. But he had kidnapped his employer's little girl, a lovely, trusting child who thought the sun, the moon and the stars all shone out of Gavin Calder.

'Bella!' Sally couldn't think of anything to do right then but call her cousin. 'Bella!'

'Cripes, Sally!' Bella sounded as shocked as she was. 'I saw it, too! You've just got to phone the police.'

Sally felt numb. She knew phoning the police was the right thing to do under the circumstances, but there was something about that that bothered her, something that didn't ride right in her. Whatever Gavin was, there was no getting away from the fact that he worshipped little Anna and the feeling was mutual. What kind of kidnapper did that make him?

'Oh, Bella! Gavin isn't some hardened criminal. He cares. He cares for Anna. That little girl wouldn't cling to any man who wasn't worth his salt.'

'Sal, baby,' Bella said in a soothing voice, but this time it didn't work its usual magic on Sally. 'You never should have got yourself involved in the first place, but I beg you, phone the police. You've got to, for your own sake. If anything happens to Anna you're never going to live with your conscience. Phone the police and let them sort things out. Please, sweetie, do it!'

Sally hung up and sat staring into space, trying to assimilate her feelings, trying to persuade herself that what Bella advised was the right thing to do. Eventually, she got up, reached for her coat and bag and headed for the door. She had no way of reaching Gavin. He had always been the one to contact her and wouldn't divulge his telephone number, even when she asked, making the excuse that he was always on the move and it was easier for him to phone her at regular intervals.

Oh, how he had deceived her.

'Where is she?'

Sally heard the outburst as she staggered back into the flat. On opening the door, Gavin Calder had burst in looking like a bomb about to go off.

'What are you talking about? How

would I know where she is? You're the kidnapper, not me!' Sally exclaimed angrily.

She saw the way his face paled at her acid words spat hatefully at him.

'What are you talking about? Sally! Talk to me! What do you know?'

He pushed her inside and shut the door behind him. He grabbed hold of her and his fingers dug into the flesh of her upper arms like steel clamps.

'Tell me!' he shouted in her face.

'The news,' she said and glanced over her shoulder at the now silent, blank screen of the television set. 'They said Anna had been kidnapped six weeks ago and that you were the chief suspect in the case. The parents had kept quiet in case of reprisals. They had been waiting for a ransom demand, but none had come, so they had approached the police.'

'And you believed that garbage? Sally, you're more of a fool than I took you for.'

'I didn't think you took me for any kind of fool, Gavin,' Sally said in a small, faltering voice. 'I thought you cared.'

Gavin's eyes closed and he swept a hand over his face as if to wipe away the tiredness that she could see gathered there.

'I trusted you, but it seems that nobody can be trusted these days. How much did they pay you, Sally?' he said in almost a whisper.

'What?'

'How much did they pay you to kidnap Anna for them?'

'I don't know what you're talking about! I haven't seen Anna since you took her away from here the night somebody tried to steal her from the park.'

He stared at her, blinking.

'Is that the truth, Sally?'

'Damn you, Gavin! Of course, it's the truth!'

She saw Gavin's throat muscles tense, saw his eyes mist over then become jet black and cold as ice.

'She was last seen talking to JoJo the Clown in the park. She got into his car, went with him willingly. Went with you!' he exclaimed.

Sally shook her head.

'No, Gavin. It wasn't me. I didn't do the JoJo thing today. I was here at The Rose Carousel all day. Ask Bella. Ask anybody in the shop. We were run off our feet. I decided that we could afford to give up JoJo for at least one day, even if it did disappoint a few children.'

'Rob, then? His brother — what's his name — Bruce?'

'Rob has his foot in plaster and Bruce called in sick. He has a dose of summer flu and I must say he sounded rough on the phone.'

'But she was seen talking to JoJo. The description was spot on, the white wig, the blue and yellow hat with a pompom, the blue, yellow and red costume and the big shiny black shoes.'

'Gavin, who was she with when she was taken?'

'The blasted nanny again, but it happened under the nose of two of my best operatives who were tailing them.'

'Then shouldn't you be investigating the nanny at least, or your own staff?'

'How many JoJo costumes are there?'

'I bought two and they were the only two in the shop. Fortunately, the big one fits Rob and the small one fits me. There were other clown costumes, but they were the only two matching ones and I did foresee the problem of having to replace Rob at some time or another, so I bought the second costume as a spare, never really thinking I'd be the one to use it.'

'Show me! Show me the costumes. Where do you keep them?'

Sally licked her lips. She ought to feel wary. Gavin had been presented on the television as a suspected kidnapper, possibly dangerous, and here she was alone with him. But she didn't get any dangerous vibes — angry ones, frustrated ones, anxious ones, but not dangerous.

'They're kept in the staffroom downstairs.'

'Show me!' Gavin repeated, gripping her wrist as if he was afraid she might try to escape him.

She took him downstairs and entered The Rose Carousel by the steel safety door that opened out on to the back yard. It could be opened easily from inside, but needed a stout key to open it from the exterior. There were only three keys in existence. Sally held one, the security alarm firm held the second and the third was lodged with the local fire brigade.

'Any more smoking men lurking in your back yard?' Gavin wanted to know, looking furtively around as he waited to gain access to the shop

'No. I never saw him again, but it was pretty scary just that once.'

'I posted one of my men in the lane after you reported that.'

'And?'

'Nothing.'

'Probably a local burglar chancing his luck.'

'Probably.'

The staffroom door was also locked, but as soon as Sally opened it and stepped inside she saw what she had feared. Rob's JoJo costume was missing.

'How many people have the key to the staffroom door?' Gavin asked.

Sally drew in breath and let it out on a long sigh.

'We all have one. It's necessary. The door has to be kept locked during the day to stop curious children and odd customers going in. The members of my staff feel they can leave their belongings in here safely. You'd be surprised at how many light-fingered people there are about these days.'

'Tell me about it!' Gavin was rubbing madly at the back of his neck. 'I have a bad feeling about this, Sally. I think we'd better pay a call on your friend, Rob.'

'You can't possibly believe that Rob has anything to do with kidnapping Anna. Nothing you say will convince me that he's the guilty party.'

'Sally, I checked up on this so-called friend of yours. I called the hospitals, all the doctors and clinics I could find in the area. Nobody had heard of Rob Barlow, except the Psychiatry Department at The General Hospital. But then, he wouldn't go there with a broken foot, would he?'

'Well, maybe Rob just wanted some time off, time to spend with his brother. I gather they haven't seen one another in a long time. If they had problems in the past they would need time to talk, time to get their act together.'

'Act is probably the right word for what they're doing, Sally. They're part of a kidnapping ring and Anna is their victim.'

'That's ridiculous!'

'Oh, is it? Is it? I checked up on brother Bruce, too. There's no record of Rob ever having had a brother. He had an older sister who died when he was a kid. No brothers.'

Sally's brow creased into a deep frown. She shook her head in disbelief. It wasn't like Rob to lie to her. And yet there had been something in his manner lately, something she just couldn't figure out something that bothered her, and it all seemed to stem from the so-called broken foot and the arrival in Rob's life of Bruce, the brother that never was.

'I have to find Anna.'

Gavin was looking more and more weighed down by concern, his emotions showing with every move, every glance. Suddenly he turned, and banged a fist against the door jamb.

'Godammit! It can't end like this. They can't take her away from me!'

'Gavin?' Sally said as a thought began to take shape in her mind.

It was there. The clue. The thing that had been locked at the back of Sally's mind. For a security chief, Gavin had too many feelings.

'Gavin, tell me the truth, please!'

He shot her a glance, then wiped a weary hand over worried eyes.

'I am who I say I am, Sally. There's no mystery there. My security firm is well established and we've been employed by the Macey family for many years. Anna is not the daughter of my millionaire employer, however. He's just her stepfather.'

His face twisted with revulsion as he spoke.

'He's a swine of the first order, but Anna's mother saw him as a good catch and he wanted an heir. He'd had three wives and no children. Not a happy state for a rich man known for his sexual prowess. Nadine planned it all down to the last detail. She was Lorn Macey's secretary and already involved with him. When she discovered his childless state she decided to get pregnant. The father of her child, whom she chose very carefully, never guessed that he was being used as a kind of surrogate. He lost out to the Macey wealth and power.'

He paused slightly for breath.

'Macey married her, but when Anna was three, Nadine walked out, or was thrown out. I was never sure one way or the other, but I can guess. She left Anna behind. Mind you, she wasn't a good mother. She treated the poor kid like a doll rather than a human being. As soon as Anna started to show some character and independence, Nadine lost interest. She was also bitterly jealous of the attention her millionaire husband gave to his stepdaughter.'

'Jealous?' Sally's brows wrinkled. 'I would have thought she was glad to find a man to love her child.'

'It depends what kind of love it is, Sally. He started abusing Anna. I didn't see it and those who did kept it to themselves because they didn't want to lose their jobs. Then, a few weeks ago, somebody found the courage to come to me and spill the beans on this rich, worldly benefactor admired by all.'

Gavin hesitated, obviously finding it

116

difficult to find the right words.

'Go on,' Sally encouraged and he gave a small nod.

'I had always been close to Anna, made it my business to look after her when I could. Things were always good between us, thank goodness, but lately I had noticed that something was wrong. Of course, she couldn't speak for herself.'

Sally swallowed hard.

'What did you do when you found out?'

'Faced him with it, at first. He just laughed. Said nobody would believe me. In public he was the perfect, loving father, and what was more, Nadine had agreed to go back to him and be a proper mother to Anna. He was paying her highly enough to do it, so she had agreed to return to the fold and turn a blind eye. This was too much for me. I took Anna and I ran. One or two of my most trusted operatives came with me to help, but things were getting too difficult and I was in danger of losing

Anna, and not for the first time.'

'What do you mean, Gavin?'

Sally thought she knew, but she wanted to hear him say it, wanted to read the depth of his feelings in his eyes as he spoke the words.

Gavin's eyes were moist as he looked up and there was a definite tremor in his voice as he confirmed what she was already beginning to suspect.

'Sally, Anna is my daughter. I've got to get her back or die in the attempt.'

# 8

'So you really did kidnap Anna?' Sally asked as she accompanied Gavin as he drove at breakneck speed across town.

They were heading for Rob's flat and somewhere in the evening traffic there were at least two other security men coming to their chief's aid. He had phoned in while driving with one hand, giving quite a few motorists, plus Sally, minor heart attacks as he zipped around them.

He nodded and the grin he gave her was tinged with a sadness she could well understand. She knew what he stood to lose, whatever the outcome. Lorn Macey was rich enough and powerful enough to challenge the law and win. Gavin could end up seeing his little daughter being handed over to a mother who, for the promise of riches, would give up her child to a monster.

'Slow down! You'll get us both killed, Gavin!'

But he wasn't in the mood to take advice. He had the Devil pushing him from behind.

'There! Next turning on the right. Straight ahead now, first left over the crossroads and watch for the . . . red light!'

There was no answer to Gavin's pressure on the doorbell of Rob's flat, or to his fist hammering on the thin, wooden panel.

'Rob! Rob, it's me, Sally! Please open the door. We've got to talk!' Sally shouted through the door, but all she got was the silence from within and Gavin's laboured breathing as he seethed impatiently by her side.

'Good evening!'

A small, polite voice made them jump and when they swivelled round they found that the owner was a short, comfortably-built man in his seventies who was regarding them with unbridled interest from the flat opposite.

'Can I help you? You know, I don't think there's anybody at home in number seven. It's been very quiet for some time.'

'Look, old man.'

Gavin went to the old fellow and laid a hand on the padded shoulder that was no higher than his own waist.

'This is an official emergency. I've got to gain access to this flat. You wouldn't have a spare key, would you?'

'Oh, no!'

The man shook his head violently and his smooth, rosy cheeks vibrated with the action.

'He would never trust me with a key. Too nosey, you know, I am. It's quite true and I'm the first to admit it, but then I always say that God gave me a nose and meant me to use it.'

'So you don't have the key, Mister . . . ?'

'Arthur.'

'Mr Arthur.'

'Just Arthur, dear boy.'

'OK, Arthur. Look, this is very important and . . . '

121

'You're American, aren't you? Why don't you do like they do in the movies? Go on, let me see you do it. Kick down the door.'

He lifted his foot as he spoke and went through the motions of a lethal kick-boxing step, nearly overbalancing in the attempt. Gavin looked from the old man to Sally, then glowered at the door. Sally saw him take a deep breath just before his foot lashed out and the door splintered. Sally pressed her hand to her mouth.

The old man was rubbing his hands together and laughing heartily, totally entertained.

'My dear girl, don't stop him now. Isn't this exciting? Do you mind if I come in with you? He's never invited me in, you know.'

Sally nodded over her shoulder as she followed close behind Gavin, picking her way delicately over the caved-in door. Arthur bumped into her as she stopped suddenly, watching Gavin's face as he reached down and picked up a small red shoe.

Sally recognised the shoe instantly. They were Anna's favourite shoes. She had worn them often.

She watched Gavin turn it around and around in his hands, saw the agitated twitch of the muscle in his cheek.

'Oh, that must belong to the little girl,' Arthur said as he came forward and pointed to the shoe. 'Pretty little thing, she was.'

'You saw her?' Gavin demanded and Arthur flinched nervously. 'You saw a little girl here in this flat? Come on, old man! This is a matter of life and death.'

'Oh, my goodness! Well, there was a little girl here this morning. She came with a tall, rather ugly-looking fellow. The poor little thing wasn't at all happy. I got the impression that she was afraid.'

'Where was Rob in all this?' Sally wanted to know. 'Was he here with them?'

'No, but I know he hadn't left the flat

at that point, and he didn't leave later after the woman arrived.'

'Woman? What woman?'

Gavin was sounding more and more threatening and the old man's chin began to quiver.

'A fancy-looking piece, all blonde and big jewellery.'

'Nadine!' Gavin muttered.

'Good-looking, some might say,' Arthur went on, 'but she had a hard face beneath all that make-up. The three of them left together half an hour later. I got the feeling that the little girl was an unwilling passenger, though she never uttered a word.'

'What car? Did you see the car?' Gavin persisted and Sally took hold of Arthur's arm and gave it an encouraging squeeze, which won her a grateful smile.

'Yes, of course I saw the car. Why, that's my hobby. From my window I make a note of all the cars I see during the day. The car the woman was driving was a metallic green BMW and if you'll just come across to my flat for a second I'll give you the registration. Good heavens! What was that?' he added in disbelief.

They all spun around at the sound of a groan and a hollow thump coming from the bedroom.

'It's coming from the wardrobe!' Sally said as a second thump came.

It was followed by a third and a fourth and further groans that were beginning to sound more like muffled words now that their attention was riveted on them.

Gavin crossed the room in two great strides and yanked open the wardrobe door. Sally gasped and ran forward as a very crumpled Rob rolled out on to the carpeted floor.

He was gagged and tied and looking positively purple in the face from lack of oxygen and the effort to free himself.

'Oh, Rob!'

Sally was fumbling with his fastenings, but was pushed aside by Gavin who tore off the broad sticky tape that was keeping him quiet and almost suffocating him after the length of time it had been in place.

'Poor boy!' Arthur murmured and went off to explore the kitchen, announcing his intention of making a pot of tea.

'Who's he?'

Rob looked from Gavin to Sally with round, worried eyes.

'Never mind who I am,' Gavin barked at him, making him blink. 'You're going to have some explaining to do to the police later about aiding and abetting kidnappers. Now, tell me what you know, and as quickly as possible.'

'All right, anything you say, but get me out of these ropes.'

'First, the answers!'

Sally bit her lip as she saw Rob wince. He wasn't the most courageous of souls at the best of times, but she felt utterly sorry for him now. He had been cruelly used and Gavin was prolonging his agony.

'Who was this Bruce fellow? He wasn't your brother, was he?' Gavin asked straight away.

Rob shook his head.

'No. I don't know him, but he made me do it. He was the one who invented the story about my broken foot. He threatened to do all sorts of things to the kids at The Rose Carousel if I didn't do what he told me. I believed him. He was rotten to the core, that one.'

Rob's voice cracked and he turned his face away so they couldn't see his tears. Sally got down on her knees and hugged him tightly.

'It's all right, Rob. You're safe now.'

She looked up at Gavin's stern face and saw no mercy.

'Well, aren't you going to cut him free?'

'There's no time for that. The old man can do it when we've gone,' Gavin replied abruptly.

'Where are we going?'

'After Nadine and her boyfriend, who

is undoubtedly one of Macey's hench-
men. At least we have a description of
the car. Arthur!'

Arthur appeared in the kitchen door,
teapot in hand.

'Any idea where the car was heading?' Gavin asked.

'North, dear boy! I'm afraid that's all
I know.'

'You've done just great, fella!'

Gavin forced his mouth into the
semblance of a grateful smile and Sally
relaxed a little, seeing the human being
coming back into the mean machine.

'Release Rob here, will you? Then I
want you both to give all this
information to the police,' Gavin was
now saying.

He took a card out of his pocket and
handed it over.

'This is the person to contact.'

'The police!'

Sally was running after him as he
bounded down the stairs and out into
the street.

'But Gavin, won't that cause trouble

for you? Gavin, you kidnapped a child. You'll go to prison!'

'Get in!' Gavin ordered as he hurriedly pulled open the passenger door of his car.

She did as he said and he slammed the door shut then got in behind the wheel. The car seemed to take off instantly, tyres screaming and gears grinding.

'Isn't there some other way?'

'I'm past worrying what they do to me. I just want to make sure that Anna doesn't land back in the hands of that pervert. You understand that, don't you, Sally?'

Of course she understood. He was a father who loved his daughter. He couldn't stand back and let her life be ruined, physically and mentally. He had to do what he had to do and she was right there with him.

'What do you want me to do, Gavin?'

'There's a map there in the pocket beside you. Take it out and find the main route north to Scotland. There's a place called Glen Tor just north of Dumfries. You can map-read, can't you? I've driven there once before, but it was a few years ago.'

'How do you know where they're headed?'

'I don't. I'm just taking a guess and following my gut feelings. Macey has a hunting lodge up there on the edge of the moors. It's his private hideaway.'

'Lucky man!'

'He won't be lucky when I get my hands on him.'

'Just promise me one thing, Gavin. Promise me you'll be very, very careful. I don't want to . . . '

Goodness, she was about to blurt out something like not wanting to lose him, but that was hardly the kind of thing to say in the circumstances. After all, they didn't really have a relationship, did they? It had almost started, but had been curtailed before getting beyond the basics. Besides, what would have been the point in starting a relationship with a man like Gavin Calder? He wasn't even from her world.

'You don't want to what?'

He glanced at her swiftly, then turned his concentration back to the busy road ahead.

'Oh, nothing. I just don't want Anna to end up visiting you in prison.'

His hand sneaked out and squeezed her thigh. She nearly choked on her emotion. Instead, she took a deep breath and hurriedly found the place he wanted on the map. It seemed a pretty straightforward route, to Dumfries at least.

What they were going to do when they got to his place that Gavin knew about, this hunting lodge, heaven only knew. Sally was aware of her heart pumping at a quickened rate and her blood racing through her veins. The nearer to Scotland they got, the worse it became. Fear and excitement made a heady cocktail.

★ ★ ★

It was already dark as they reached Dumfries. Gavin negotiated heavy traffic through the town centre, then they headed north.

'You can put that map away now, Sally,' Gavin told her softly and in the dark she felt his fingers squeeze her hand. 'Well done. We've made it.'

'Oh, it wasn't that difficult,' she said, feeling her face flush red and glad he couldn't see it.

'No, but you made it easier for me. Thanks.'

'What about the rest of the journey?'

'It's not detailed on the map, but I think I can remember the way from here.'

'I hope so, and I hope your gut feeling is right, about them being there, I mean.'

He tossed her a tight little smile that was picked up in the headlights of an oncoming car.

'Me, too.'

# 9

'So what do we do now?' Sally whispered hoarsely as Gavin switched off the car headlights and the engine.

They were sitting outside a low, log cabin that had been constructed more like a small mansion and must look, Sally thought, very attractive in the daylight. Right now it looked dark and sinister, apart from one small chink of light that escaped through the heavy drapes at the main window.

'You stay here while I go in.'

'I'm coming, too!'

'I'm not having you put yourself in danger on my account.'

'Who said it was on your account? I'm thinking of Anna. Anyway, I helped you find the place!'

'I still want you to stay here where you're safe.'

The car they had been hoping to see,

the metallic green BMW, was parked outside the main entrance towards which Gavin was now heading. He moved stealthily on trained feet and Sally felt her heart lurch uncomfortably as he reached the door and looked back at the car where she was still sitting. He was obviously checking to make sure she had stayed put.

As soon as he disappeared, which told her that the cabin door had been left carelessly ajar, she got out of the car and went after him. Her trainers crunched slightly on the gravel, but she could already hear loud music coming from inside the lodge. Somebody liked traditional jazz and liked it hot.

Gavin was just inside the hallway when she slid in. He spun around, ready to attack or defend himself, but then seeing it was Sally, he tossed his eyes to the ceiling and motioned to her to be quiet.

Keeping close behind him, masked by his bulk, Sally crept forward with Gavin, every step of the way. When he pulled up abruptly at the partly-open door that was spilling out bright light, she bumped into him. One of his hands came back and thrust her against the wall, his body pinning her there for an instant. Then he released her, pulled her forward and nodded towards the light.

She peered in curiously, fearfully, then drew back with a gasp. Inside the room, which was sumptuously furnished, a couple was embracing before a roaring, open fire. Their bodies swayed to the rhythm of the background music.

It was the woman Arthur had described to them, and her partner was none other than Bruce, the man she had thought to be Rob's brother. Nadine, Anna's mother, appeared to be making a meal of him.

Gavin put his mouth close to Sally's ear and whispered, 'Behold the mother of my child, and her new playmate.'

Just then, Nadine broke away from Bruce and they could see Anna sitting huddled in the corner of a sofa, her face full of misery, her eyes full of hate and fear as she clutched a cushion to her and watched the two people who had abducted her.

Nadine had her bag now and was pulling out a thick envelope, which she handed over to Bruce. He gave a snake-like grin and opened it, taking out a wad of bank notes that even from where Sally stood looked like a small fortune.

'For services rendered, big boy!' Nadine said, throwing back her head and laughing. 'Now you can go.'

She jabbed a well-manicured finger into the man's chest and indicated the door with a jerk of her head. He looked reluctant to move at first, but she jabbed again and her expression became instantly ugly and menacing.

'OK, OK! Thanks for the dough!'

He waved the wad of notes beneath her nose, laughed, then headed for where Gavin and Sally were standing. Sally felt herself being almost lifted bodily from her position to the other side of the door and as Bruce came through, Gavin's fist shot out in a fast uppercut that looked too good to be real. Bruce was instantly felled. He slithered to the floor with a mildly surprised grunt and lay there.

Gavin stepped into the room and faced Nadine, who was trying to decide how to arrange her face for best effect. Sally stepped over the comatose Bruce and came to Gavin's side, which earned her a look of stupefaction from Nadine.

There was a sudden commotion from behind Nadine as Anna recognised the two newcomers. She slithered off the sofa and shot across the room, ending up hugging Gavin's knees, tears washing over her pale cheeks, sobs racking her fine frame.

'Hi, baby! You're going to be just fine. Go to Sally, sweetheart. Let her look after you, eh?'

He pushed her gently across to Sally, who kneeled down and hugged the little girl and felt her throat tighten as Anna hugged her back.

'So, who's your girlfriend, Gavin?' Nadine asked, head to one side, hand on one tilted hip.

Sally could see how the woman could fool any man into thinking she was beautiful and desirable but it was skin deep. Not far beneath the attractive veneer she was ice cold and ugly and right now it was showing through. Sally wondered how long it had taken Gavin to find out. Not long, she was sure. Right now, he was looking as mean as he could get.

'You can forget your little game, Nadine. You're not going to use Anna to get you back in favour with your pet millionaire.'

'What do you plan to do, Gavin? Kidnap her again? As far as the authorities are concerned, she's his official daughter and I'm still his wife. He wants his little family back together again. If you try to take Anna away they'll arrest you and throw you in prison. What are you, anyway, but a cheap security man! Nobody would believe your word against ours, against the official documents.'

Sally could see Gavin's jaws clench, together with his fists.

'I have the DNA evidence that Anna is my daughter. I also have evidence against your fine, upstanding husband that proves just what kind of father he is. I have eye witnesses and even one member of the family who can no longer bear to keep quiet after what they saw. And how do you think the public will react to that, and to the fact that you knew about it and didn't do anything other than run out on your own three-year-old child?'

'You can't do this to me, Gavin. You wouldn't dare.'

'Try me.'

'If you go against me I can see to it that you lose your silly security firm. You'll never work again. How would you like that?'

'It's dirty money you're living off Nadine,' Gavin said, ignoring her remarks. 'There's not an honest dollar anywhere in your husband's account and when you get back to the States I think you'll find there are certain government bodies waiting with leading questions.'

'I want my daughter!' Nadine shrieked and suddenly there was a gun in her hand, pointed, not at Gavin, but at Sally.

Sally got slowly to her feet, her heart thumping, her legs turning to jelly. She grabbed hold of Anna and pushed her behind her, shielding the child with her own body. At the same time, Gavin stepped in front of Sally and spread his arms in supplication.

'No guns, Nadine. That way people get hurt, killed maybe.'

Sally tugged at Gavin's jacket.

'Gavin, be careful. She's crazy.'

'Crazy, am I?' Nadine hissed her words. 'Yes, maybe I am, but then, wouldn't you be crazy if you saw a multi-million dollar deal being flushed down the tubes. Send the kid over here.

I want Anna over here, now!'

The gun was wavering in her hand, but even from across the room, Sally could see that the woman was pulling on the trigger. It could go off at any moment and Gavin would die, then it would be her turn.

'Put the gun down, Nadine!' Gavin whispered.

The explosion took them all by surprise. Even Nadine herself, who had pulled the trigger, recoiled, her face as white as parchment. Sally clung desperately to Anna behind Gavin's back.

'Anna, get over here or I'll kill your friends, honey!'

Nadine had recovered and was calling out to Anna, who immediately pulled away from Sally and went towards her mother before Sally could stop her.

'You know I'll do it, don't you? Remember your dog!'

The child's face twisted with mental agony as she placed herself at Nadine's side.

'You were never an animal lover, Nadine,' Gavin said. 'Any more than you loved children. How you and your millionaire have tortured Anna.'

Sally noticed that his voice was strained and he was clutching at his arm where a dark red stain was slowly seeping through his jacket.

'Gavin, you're hurt!' she whispered.

'I'll survive,' he told her quickly. 'It's only a flesh wound.'

Sally was enraged. She turned on the woman with the gun.

'You bitch! What kind of woman are you, anyway?'

'A desperate one, honey,' Nadine said in a low voice, then her face locked rigid as another person joined them, someone who had entered by the back door and had possibly been listening to the entire conversation.

'Give me the gun, Nadine. You're frightening our visitors.'

The soft, velvety tones held all the menace it needed to reduce Nadine to a quivering mass. She turned and looked

142

at the short, stocky figure who had come up behind her and the gun went limp in her hand.

'Lorn!'

Nadine seemed to shrink before him.

'I was only doing it for you, so you could have your daughter back. You always said how your life was lacking without children. I'm your wife, so that makes Anna your daughter, right?'

'Wrong.'

The man took the gun from his wife's hand and placed it in his pocket, then he turned his attention to Gavin and Sally.

'I'm too old to have young children around me. Take your daughter, Calder, and your pretty lady friend. Take them and go. All business between you and me is terminated. I never want to see hide nor hair of you again.'

'I think you'll find that a little difficult, Macey. No doubt we'll meet again, in court.'

'Only if you can find me, Calder. This isn't my only hideaway. There are others, far more discreet than this one. Take your little family and forget about me.'

He turned and fixed Nadine with a stony stare.

'That includes you, sweetheart. Take her with you, Calder. She's no more use to me. And she's acted foolishly with this latest ruse to trap me.'

Gavin glanced at Sally, smiled through his pain and shook his head.

'No, Macey, you keep her. You deserve one another, it seems to me.'

Then he looked at his daughter and his smile became warmer.

'Come on, Anna. Let's go.'

Anna flung herself at him for the second time that evening, her face wreathed in happy smiles. She grabbed his coat sleeve, not noticing how he winced as she dragged him to the open door. Then she turned and held out her soft, baby hand to Sally.

'Sally!' she said. 'Come on, Sally. You, too!'

Anna had spoken!

Gavin's eyes met and locked with Sally's. They looked glassy and she realised that they were swimming with unshed tears. She remembered how he told her that Anna had not spoken a word for about two years, ever since her mother ran off and left her with her evil stepfather.

'Yes, I'm coming, Anna,' Sally said.

She swallowed the lump that had arisen in her throat and took Anna's hand in hers. Together they left the lodge and walked slowly back to the car where Gavin called up his team of operatives on his mobile and gave them the location.

He then contacted the police. His conversation was short and brief and it was obvious that they had not been ignorant of what was going on.

'Why didn't you bring them in earlier?' Sally asked.

'Selfishness, I suppose,' he told her, brushing her cheek with the back of his good hand. 'I wanted to be in on the kill.'

'They knew you had Anna, didn't they?'

Sally stared into the darkness, feeling Anna's sleepy head getting heavier as the little girl nestled against her in the back seat of the car.

'Yes. I've been working with them to get evidence against Lorn Macey. They want him out of the country, so I guess he'll be expedited back to the States and there'll be quite a reception committee waiting for him there. He's not exactly Mister Nice Guy in America, the UK or anywhere else. Not any more.'

Sally felt her spirits sag slightly as a thought struck her.

'So, no more work here for Calder Security Enterprises.'

There was a short pause before he replied, 'No, I guess not.'

'Will you be going back to the States? You and Anna?'

'I guess we have to go back, yes. There's a bit of unfinished business before this affair can be put behind us.

And, of course, I have to see about finding a home for Anna and myself. Maybe I'll take some time off from business and just occupy myself with my daughter's welfare for a while.'

'Her mother won't try to get her back, will she?'

'No chance. Nadine only wanted to use Anna as a tool to pry a few million away from her rich husband.'

Gavin reached over the back of his seat and gently stroked his sleeping daughter's dark head.

'I stuck around as best I could to make sure she was all right and I think she was for a while. Then Nadine bolted, took off with a younger man. She always was one for having a good time and Macey didn't come up to scratch. I don't know why she came back. It doesn't matter now. If she hadn't, I wouldn't have known about the child cruelty. It was a friend of hers who told me about it. And then, when I looked further into things I found he had a history of that kind of thing going back some. I knew I wouldn't be able to get custody overnight, so I took matters into my own hands.'

Sally sighed.

'You could still be in trouble with the authorities, Gavin, for what you did. You might even go to prison.'

'It's possible, but I don't think that will happen, not now. We have too many witnesses. I expect your friend, Rob, will also give evidence.'

Sally licked her lips and thought how scared poor Rob had looked, but how proud he would be to be able to help Anna and her true father to get together finally. The child stirred in her arms and she hugged her close, glad that it was too dark for Gavin to see the tears in her eyes.

'You really do love her, don't you?' she said with a little break in her voice.

'I think she's the greatest kid that ever lived,' Gavin told her. 'And I hope she'll have a bevy of brothers and sisters one day.'

'I never thought I'd ever hear a man

say that,' Sally said, burying her face in Anna's hair, struggling with feelings of envy and regret, and wondering if there was another man like Gavin somewhere, because it would be so easy to fall in love with him.

'Here they come,' Gavin said, jerking up straight in his seat and watching a procession of car headlights approaching from the distance.

'So, it's all over bar the shouting,' Sally said dully and felt Gavin look at her through the darkness.

'Yes, I daresay you could be right.'

The silence fell heavy between them.

# 10

Sally gazed out of the window and thought there was something very special about a white Christmas. Everything outside was crisp and glistening and fluffy white snowflakes were fluttering down from a clear iced blue sky.

The doorbell jangled and she heard Bella greeting people, heard the stamping of feet as they shook off the snow, the jovial greetings and the rustle of wrapping paper on the gifts they carried.

For a moment it was all in the hazy distance, because Sally's thoughts were sailing across the Atlantic to a small house with a well-established rose garden, which was how Gavin's letter had described his and Anna's new home.

There was a photograph stuck up on

the notice board of Anna standing proudly before the white-painted picket fence.

Sally wondered what kind of Christmas Day they were celebrating over there in the States and if Gavin would have a thought for her as Anna opened the present of a JoJo musical clown she had sent.

'Merry Christmas, Sally!'

Rob, his face glowing pink with the cold, his eyes shining happily, came and gave her a hug.

'This is Stephen. You said I could bring somebody. I hope you don't mind.'

'Of course not. Merry Christmas, Rob, Stephen, and make yourselves at home.'

She shook hands with Rob's new partner and decided she liked the look of him. He had honest eyes and a nice smile.

'I'll just go and put the finishing touches to the punch.'

'Hope it's hot and spicy like you usually make!'

Rob unwound a scarf from his neck and stood, rubbing his hands together.

'Hot, spicy and very alcoholic.'

Sally laughed.

'Bella knocked my elbow as I was pouring in the rum. She said it was an accident.'

'Well, you don't have to believe me if you don't want to,' Bella called out from the kitchen where she was basting the turkey.

Everything was prepared. Despite feeling sad around the edges, Sally had been determined to have a jolly, family Christmas with Bella and Rob and a couple of the girls who worked for her and, like her, didn't have anywhere else to go at the festive season. And, of course, she had invited Arthur, Rob's next-door neighbour, who had since become a very good friend.

Jane and Linda were stacking presents under the Christmas tree while nibbling on crisps and nuts and generally enjoying themselves, like excited children. It was just a pity that there weren't any children present, because that was what made Christmas real, Sally always thought.

She had wondered about throwing the shop open just for the afternoon, but it wouldn't have been fair on the staff needed to run things.

However, she had lit the place up and set off the carousel which was now playing seasonal carols to lend a little magic to the Christmas atmosphere.

'Let's take the punch and the nibbles downstairs,' she decided suddenly and Bella looked at her as if she was quite mad. 'I want to hear the music better. I want to see the coloured lights and the horses going round and round.'

'All right! All right! I'm convinced. Everybody downstairs!' Bella shouted to one and all.

They had closed off the backyard area as an added security precaution. The work had been finished last week and Sally felt a lot safer.

She had stopped looking out of her bedroom window expecting to see the glow of a cigarette every night after dark. That, of course, had been Bruce, the bogus brother of Rob, who was now doing a short stretch in prison for his part in the affair. And back in the States, Lorn Macey and Nadine were doing a much longer stretch between them. The authorities had, for once, been on the ball and moved in before the couple had a chance to disappear.

Gavin's name, of course, had been cleared. With Macey safe behind bars there was no end of witnesses speaking out against him.

'Sally! Hey! Where are you?'

Sally swung around, not sure which one of the girls had called out to her.

'Sorry?'

She had been standing in front of the carousel, her mind a million miles away, her heart feeling like a heavy brick inside her.

'Linda and I are opting to open prezzies now, with the punch,' Jane said and the others nodded in total accord.

'Anything you say.'

Sally smiled at them all, feeling a warm glow creep over her. She really must pull herself together and get on with her life. Gavin was history. She just wished he was long-past history, instead of something that was still close enough to touch her, close enough to hurt. Linda suddenly grabbed her and gave her a sisterly hug.

'It's really super of you to have us here today and it's — oh, everything is so wonderful and . . . '

She looked close to tears.

'Oh, for goodness' sake, don't! We'll all be crying buckets if you go on like that!'

Bella gave the girl an affectionate push and was about to say something to Sally when a sudden rattling at the shop door made them all look in that direction.

'Hey, look!'

Rob pointed at a small figure and a face pressed up against the glass of the door.

'Is that who I think it is, Sally?'

Sally took a step or two forward, not believing her eyes. It was difficult to be sure, since the small girl was muffled up in clothes to keep out the winter chill and was sprinkled liberally with snow.

'Sally!'

She heard the child's high voice penetrating the reinforced doubleglazing, saw the dark eyes widening, the pretty face dimpling into a huge smile.

'Anna? Anna, is that you?'

She unlocked the door and pulled it wide.

'What on earth?'

Anna almost fell in upon her, hugging her tightly. Snowflakes billowed in through the open doorway. Then a movement to the side caught Sally's attention.

She looked up and saw Gavin standing there in the street, tall, dark and handsome, and he was looking at her with such an intense expression in his wonderful eyes and an uncertain smile playing about his mouth.

'Gavin!' she exclaimed.

'May we come in, Sally?'

Sally blinked snow from her eye-lashes, shivered and stepped back into the shop, aware that her friends were all gathering around her, full of curiosity.

'Of course you can! Goodness, you must be frozen standing out there like that. I — er — I think you've probably met everybody — er — except Stephen.'

'I hope we're not disturbing a family gathering.'

Gavin brushed snow from his broad shoulders as Sally left Rob to close the door behind him.

She didn't seem too capable of functioning right now. Her legs and brain had turned to jelly.

'You're more than welcome,' Bella said and stood on tiptoe to help Gavin remove his coat.

Her eyes were big and shining and her thin eyebrows were almost out of control as she made frantic signals to Sally from behind the big American's back.

'Isn't he, Sally? The little one, too. We've missed her — both of you — eh, Sally?'

'Er — yes.'

'I'm glad to hear it.'

Gavin's mouth twitched and a spark of humour shot into his eyes, then he rubbed his hands together and sniffed the air.

'Is that hot rum punch I can smell?'

Sally turned back to the punch, filled a glass with the steamy, spicy liquid and held it out to him. It shook discernibly and some of it spilled when he reached out and his fingers touched hers as he took it from her.

'Sorry!' she said quickly.

'Nervous?'

'Why should I be nervous?'

'I don't know. Why should you?'

They fell silent then, looking at one another and it was all old memories and seeing things for the first time and Sally's knees were beginning to give way beneath her.

'Sally! Sally! Where's JoJo?'

Anna was tugging at her, dancing with excitement, her eyes round like saucers, her cheeks dimpled and rosy.

'JoJo?'

Sally recovered some equilibrium and glanced around her.

'Well, I don't know, Anna. You know, even clowns get time off at Christmas. Maybe Rob could go and look for him. It's just possible he hasn't gone home to Clownland yet.'

Sally raised her eyebrows at Rob, who got the message and disappeared smartly into the staffroom.

'Is there really a place called Clownland?'

Anna was ecstatic with this new knowledge.

'Well, of course! Clowns go home to Clownland and Santa goes home to Santaland and . . . '

'Do you believe in Santa Claus, Sally?'

The little girl looked doubtful.

'Nadine told me that he doesn't really exist and that it's all a silly story to fool children and make them appear stupid.'

'My goodness, Anna, that's a big sentence for such a little girl!'

Sally laughed and caught Gavin's eye. He was watching her and his daughter with an expression she hoped she wasn't mistaking.

'I believe in Clownland and Santa-land and all the people who live in them, Anna,' Sally continued. 'There are real clowns and there is certainly a real Santa Claus. He doesn't always get around to everybody, which is sad, but then it's a big world and there are lots of people, not just little children, who are making wishes out there.'

Anna considered that silently, then a smile broke out all over her pretty little face.

'I made two wishes, Sally,' she said. 'I wished that I could come back here and ride on the Rose Carousel again with you and Daddy.'

'Did you really?'

'And I made another wish, but

Daddy made me promise not to tell you, because he made the same wish and it's a great big secret, but I don't understand why.'

'Anna!' Gavin said sharply, but he was smiling. 'There's no need to give all our secrets away just yet, honey.'

Anna heaved a great sigh and looked at Sally with a very mature woman-to-woman expression on her face! At which point they were all saved from further embarrassment by the arrival of Bella and the girls bearing trays of hot canapés, which everyone fell on hungrily.

'Nice, isn't it?' Bella whispered in Sally's ear in passing. 'Just like a family Christmas ought to be.'

'It's pretty close,' Sally agreed, watching with a swelling heart as Gavin bent down to have a private chat with his daughter.

They looked so good together she wanted to cry.

'Hello, hello, hello! And a very Merry Christmas to one and all!'

Rob, dressed as JoJo, burst into their midst and there was much laughter, especially from Anna, who flew to join him and plant a kiss on his bulbous red nose.

His ears lit up immediately and her happy giggles were like the sound of fairy bells to Sally's ears.

'Daddy, is it all right for JoJo and me to ride the carousel?' Anna wanted to know, already pulling Rob in that direction.

'I guess it's OK, isn't it, Sally?'

Gavin was there by her side, smiling down at her and his hand was fumbling for hers and she was blushing madly.

'Yes — um — yes, of course. I'll just start it off.'

'No need, dear lady,' JoJo pronounced, holding up his big white-gloved hands. 'JoJo can do it. Now, princess, which stallion shall we ride?'

'The unicorn!'

Anna jumped up and down ecstatically, clapping her small, chubby hands together.

'Then the unicorn it is.'

Rob lifted Anna on to her mount and climbed up behind her with a wink to the others and an encouraging finger that told them to do likewise. Sally and Gavin laughed to see the whole gathering scrambling to get up on to the slowly-moving horses until there was only one horse left vacant. Even Arthur had managed to scramble aboard one of the smaller horses and was beaming merrily.

'Daddy! Sally! Come on! You, too!'

Sally glanced up at Gavin and found his eyes already on her and they seemed to be burning into her heart and mind.

'Shall we join them, Sally?' Gavin asked and she nodded, feeling her cheeks burn as he picked her up bodily and almost threw her on to the galloping white stallion with the red and gold crown and the royal blue saddle.

The carousel was gathering momentum, the music getting faster and louder. Suddenly, with one easy leap, like a cowboy mounting his horse, Gavin was there behind her, so close that they might almost be one. One arm came around her waist, while the other gripped the reins. Sally felt herself rise and fall as the carousel swept around and around. Her head was swimming, but it wasn't just because of the punch or the ride.

Gavin leaned forward, putting his face hard against hers.

'I could get used to this!' he shouted over the tinkling music. 'How about you?'

'I — I'm not sure. I need time to get acclimatised.'

'I'm prepared to wait, Sally, if you'll promise to get acclimatised to me, and to Anna.'

Sally could do nothing but breathe deeply and try to control the mad beating of her heart, which he must surely feel through the silk sweater she was wearing.

'Do I have to spell it out, Sally? We both love you, Anna and I. We both have needs that we believe you can fulfil. Now, do you understand what I'm trying to say to you?'

Sally was suddenly aware that the carousel had stopped and so had the music, yet it all still seemed to be going on in her head.

'Oh, dear!'

She laughed, a light, embarrassed sound.

'It's funny, but I could swear I'm still going around and up and down and I feel so light-headed.'

'Me, too,' Gavin murmured against her ear as his arms tightened around her from behind.

His mouth nuzzled her neck, giving her tiny, butterfly kisses.

Sally came to in a blinding flash, then realised that they were alone. The others had tactfully withdrawn to the flat upstairs. No doubt Bella and the girls were checking on the turkey and organising the first course. Stephen would be opening the champagne and JoJo would be turning himself back into

Rob. Little Anna would be waiting impatiently.

'I don't know,' Sally started to say, but Gavin had her face in his hands and was turning her so he could find her mouth and his was hungry and she had never felt like this before.

'Admit it, Sally,' he was saying against her lips. 'Admit that you felt exactly like me the first time we met. I've never wanted any woman more. Tell me you felt the same for me.'

It was Sally's turn to groan now. How could she deny it?

'Oh, yes, Gavin! Yes!'

Almost as if by magic, the hurdy-gurdy Christmas music started up again and the undulating movement of the white stallion beneath them took them soaring, higher and higher. *m*

We do hope that you have enjoyed reading this large print book.

Did you know that all of our titles are available for purchase?

We publish a wide range of high quality large print books including:
**Romances, Mysteries, Classics**
**General Fiction**
**Non Fiction and Westerns**

Special interest titles available in large print are:
**The Little Oxford Dictionary**
**Music Book, Song Book**
**Hymn Book, Service Book**

Also available from us courtesy of Oxford University Press:
**Young Readers' Dictionary**
**(large print edition)**
**Young Readers' Thesaurus**
**(large print edition)**

For further information or a free brochure, please contact us at:
**Ulverscroft Large Print Books Ltd.,**
**The Green, Bradgate Road, Anstey,**
**Leicester, LE7 7FU, England.**
**Tel:** (00 44) **0116 236 4325**
**Fax:** (00 44) **0116 234 0205**

*Other titles in the*
*Linford Romance Library:*

## VISIONS OF THE HEART

### Christine Briscomb

When property developer Connor Grant contracted Natalie Jensen to landscape the grounds of his large country house near Ashley in South Australia, she was ecstatic. But then she discovered he was acquiring — and ripping apart — great swathes of the town. Her own mother's house and the hall where the drama group met were two of his targets. Natalie was desperate to stop Connor's plans — but she also had to fight the powerful attraction flowing between them.

# DIVIDED LOYALTIES

## Phyllis Demaine

When Heather's fiancé, Adrian, is offered a wonderful job in America their future seems rosy. However, Adrian's brother, Carl, a widower, asks for Heather's help with his small, deaf son. Help which, as a speech therapist, Heather is qualified to give. But things become complicated when Carl goes abroad on business and returns with Gisel, to whom his son takes an instant dislike. This puts Heather in the position of having to choose between the boy's happiness and her own.

# THE PERFECT GENTLEMAN

## Liz Pedersen

When Laura agrees to help Anthony Christopher to deceive his family she has no idea how far the web of intrigue will extend, or how it will alter her life. His family is as unpleasant as he promised, but Laura drives away from his funeral thinking she has escaped their malicious clutches. However, this is not so. James Christopher is determined to discover what was behind his cousin's precipitate marriage. He despises Laura and hates the fact that he is attracted to her.